OLD DOG NEW TRICKS

VIVIENNE SAVAGE

PAYNE & TAYLOR

Old Dog, New Tricks
Wild Operatives #4

By Vivienne Savage

http://www.viviennesavage.com
Edited by Lindsey Loucks

1

LYLE

When you're a guy without a job, the days blend, running into one another without any point of reference. I live a perpetual case of same shit, different day, sitting on Mama's porch and wishing I'd taken a different path with my life.

Maybe I'd have a chance if I lived in a sprawling metropolis somewhere. In the big city, I'd be another anonymous, faceless ex-con. That ain't the case though. This is Quickdraw, Texas. Population 1841. Most kids graduated from high school and blew straight outta this dump without ever looking back.

Then you had dummies like me who stayed behind and ruined their lives selling dope and whatever else we could get our hands on.

Sitting on the porch with my feet propped on the rail, I placed a cigarette between my lips and plucked the lighter from the wooden rail. The screen door creaked open behind me as I lit it.

"Lyle?"

"Yeah, Ma?" I asked after the first drag.

"I hurt my shoulder last night while sleeping. Would you mind reaching up and getting this pan from the rack above the stove? I just can't get it down."

"Sure."

"Put out that cancer stick first before you come inside my house."

I sighed. Her house, her rules, so I set it aside in the ashtray, hoping to return to it after helping her. Following Mama into the kitchen was a sight for my eyes. Collard greens overflowed from the sink, part of the night's dinner. Boxes of corn meal, jars of honey, and sticks of softening butter sat on the counter.

Mama is a real southern lady. You can always count on her to use at least a whole stick of butter in whatever she's cooking.

"What all are you making?" I asked.

"Greens and ham hocks, buttered cheese biscuits, and the fried chicken you wrote home about that day. Oh, and that sweet cornbread you liked so much."

I shot a skeptical glance at the bowl of cored apples on the counter.

"And apple dumplings." Also my favorite.

My gaze darted to the bags of uncooked macaroni. Another favored side dish. "And my favorite macaroni and cheese, too, I'm guessing?"

Mama beamed proudly. "How'd you get to be so smart?" I couldn't tell if it was sarcasm.

"Why is everything stuff I like?"

My mother stepped up to me and touched her fingers to my cheek. "Because I'm so happy to have you home again, Lyle. I know I should have welcomed you back last week with a real home-cooked meal, but I just didn't have the money for it then."

My brows drew together. If she didn't have the money for it then, how the hell did she get it now? With a disabled mother in her sixties, I should have been the one looking after her, helping with her bills, giving back for the eighteen plus years she raised me, nurtured me, and helped me through life. Instead, I was just a burden on her, a mongrel she'd been stuck with after Daddy knocked her up and disappeared out of our lives.

"You don't have to do all this for me, Mama. I told you that," I told her again gently, setting my right hand on her shoulder.

Mama's gaze cut to my left arm. What was left of it anyway. Everything from two inches below my elbow was gone, lost during a life or death fight against a mean ass gator shifter from Louisiana. It was both a badge of honor and shame.

"You lost so much weight while you were away in the penitentiary, Lyle."

"Ma, I'm fifteen pounds heavier," I reminded her.

"Yeah, well, you don't look it," she shot back. She poked me in my stomach, stabbing muscle with her index finger. There used to be a thick fat pad courtesy of my old twelve-beer-a-day habit, back before I was locked up in prison.

"Ow."

"That never hurt you before."

"I had fat there before," I muttered.

"Exactly! Now get out of here so I can work."

Mama and I lived in a cramped, five-room house tucked away at the end of a long rural road. She claimed Daddy built the place with his bare hands, but since I couldn't remember meeting the son of a bitch, I had my doubts. He'd run off with his tail between his legs a little after I was born. Maybe he'd realized fatherhood was too much for him and hit the road before he could screw up.

Or maybe he was a yellow coward, and we were better off without him.

"It's hot outside," I grumbled.

"Why don't you shift and lay out on the lawn. Get some of this fresh air while we have it," Mama suggested.

"Mama, it's one hundred and three degrees outside. What fresh air?"

"You get under that shade tree, and you'll feel it." A tiny smile came to her face. "I've missed seein' you out in the yard, son. Go on. Chase a rabbit for me like you used to do when you were a kid. Find a nice, fat one, and I'll stew it tomorrow."

I'd love to do that, Mama, but I ain't got but three legs, I thought. I'd never keep pace with a rabbit, hobbling along after it. Of course, I hadn't taken my dog form since the day the gator rolled me in the dust and snapped my foreleg clean in half. I grimaced, reliving vivid memories.

Sometimes, the pain came to life again like a brand new wound, and then there were times when I'd awaken at night with tingling in my fingertips. The phantom limb sensations were a bitch.

"Okay," I agreed reluctantly.

With only two neighbors living on our street, we had all the privacy we needed. I still didn't risk shifting outside, afraid someone would wander by at the precise moment I was standing on the lawn with my dick out for the world to see. I chuckled to myself, ambling from the kitchen into the makeshift bedroom I'd claimed.

The figurative ghost of my deadbeat father still lingered in our house. I stepped over a few boxes holding old mementos from their marriage and shed my clothes, leaving them in a disorganized pile.

Dreading the shift, I stood naked in the middle of the tiny room. A pins and needles sensation traveled down the nonexistent fingers of my left hand, but I shut it out and concentrated on my animal side. As I transitioned from two legs to three limbs, ginger red fur spread over my body, mottled with white patches. With my weight balanced on my rear legs and right paw, I stretched and sniffed the air.

God, Mama's cooking smelled so damn good, and she'd barely got started. I hurried out, clumsy at first, but quickly found the rhythm to my new gait. With some stumbles, I reached the kitchen counter and eyeballed the steaming chicken legs she took from the bubbling grease. My mouth watered.

"You'll burn yourself," she warned me.

I gave her a look.

"Don't give me those puppy dog eyes, boy. Half an hour from now, you'll be in here crying and asking why I let you do it. Wait until they're cooled off." She sighed, but then her expression warmed. "Bet you're as fast as you always were, baby. Go out for a run. By the time you come back, I'll have all this ready for you."

Maybe I didn't deserve it, but I sure appreciated what she did for me.

Even though it had to hurt her to bend over the way she did, Mama leaned down and kissed me on the nose. "Go on now. Can't get a thing done with you sittin' by my feet."

She nudged again until I moved for the door, my claws clicking over hardwood floor. With a press of my head against the screen, it popped open and swung shut behind me.

A thousand smells and odors assaulted my sensitive nose, intensified by the shift to my natural state. As the wind whispered between the flower bushes, it carried the scent of the high grass, our chickens, and Mama's three outdoors cats. For a while, I was overwhelmed and unable to do anything more than breathe it all in.

After moving down the creaky old ramp that had replaced our stairs, the cool grass welcomed me into a swaying embrace, the uncut blades tickling my ribs.

For three years, I had been denied the privilege to

run wild and free. Prison sucked for anyone, but especially for shifters. Fuck, I'd lived for those rare moments outside on the recreation yard, longing for a private moment to roll in the grass.

So I took the moment now. Green blades crushed beneath my body as I rolled across the lawn. The dirt beneath was dry and itchy, but I didn't care. I'd water the yard after the sun set, not that it would do much good. Mama didn't have the strength or time to keep up our patch of land.

Eventually, the neighbors would be asking Mama when her old dog came back home, or if she'd just gone and gotten another. She'd make up something. She always did. They thought Mama was insane about coonhounds, because she always had one chasing squirrels in the yard.

When I was a kid, the guy down the road questioned why I never played with the dog or walked him. Mama fixed that by adopting two old hounds from a rescue. Over time, they became the brothers I never had.

And then one by one, they were gone. We never adopted more dogs after that.

A monstrous tow truck rumbled down the road with a shiny Subaru sedan attached. The new paint job gleamed beneath the sun in a blend of unusual colors not carried by the manufacturer. It had to be a custom job.

I picked up my head for a look at the Rave-Mobile just as a teenage girl squealed and darted from the house across the road. Wait, not a teenager. A college-age girl with mile long legs tucked into denim cutoffs. Intrigued, I leapt up to my three paws and shook out my coat before padding over to the fence.

"You fixed it!"

I recoiled when the driver stepped from the cab and promptly moved on to mind my own business. The wind carried the stench of wildcat to me the moment Taylor stepped outside.

"Told you it wasn't much of a thing to fix up."

I didn't recognize the girl until her father jogged outside with his checkbook. George Kerrington was the local butcher and sort of a legend around these parts. Or a nightmare if you were the boy trying to date his baby girl.

Hot damn. Little Lacey had grown up. Of course, the last time I'd seen her, she'd been all knees and elbows. A scrawny broomstick with a flat ass and no tits. Puberty had treated her well.

What the hell am I doin'?

A hard dose of reality made me feel like an old pervert for drooling over a chick fresh outta high school. Her dad would shoot me sooner than anything else if he caught me.

Lacey gushed over her car. Taylor's voice carried over. He explained the new additions, pointed out the finer details in the paint job, and told the girl the dos and don'ts for maintaining it all. It made me miss my days in the garage. Miss being under a car dirtied with engine grease.

If I stayed in this house, I'd drain my mom's pension to the last dollar. Somehow, I had to get back on my feet and strike out on my own again. I had to find another way. A legal way to help her the way she'd helped me.

Looking back at her overgrown yard, I knew what I had to do.

~

If I told my mom about the plans going through my head, she would have leapt from the bed, spent an hour fussing over her appearance, then driven me to town. I awakened at the crack of dawn and walked the three miles into Quickdraw instead.

I couldn't get over how much this little shit hole had changed. When Jada, Taylor's girlfriend, claimed her intent to breathe new life into our town, we'd laughed and given the woman hell at every turn. We sent our boys to smoke and litter in front of her shop. We hassled the younger brother of one of her stylists until he joined us. We did everything but break in, because T.J., at least for a while, had been one of us, and actually wrecking her joint was the cardinal sin we wouldn't commit.

Three years had changed the place.

Nirvana, Jada's salon and spa, looked bigger than I recalled, its entrance moved to the adjacent storefront. Stepping inside, I noticed a wall had been knocked down to connect Jada's original space to the new one.

An enormous sales counter awaited me at the front, manned by a woman with a jubilant smile and dark hair in wild curls to her shoulders. I didn't recognize her.

Good. That meant she wouldn't know me either.

"Can I help you, sir? Do you have an appointment?"

I shook my head. "No, ma'am. I don't…do this kind of thing."

"Why not?" She smiled again. "We have plenty of male clients."

"You got an opening for just a haircut?"

The whole time I was in the chair, I waited for someone to come out, recognize me, and glare. Or say something. Hell, I expected Jada herself to give me the boot, but it never happened. Maybe she had the day off, or she was on the other side doing one of her fancy massages. Whatever it was, I counted myself lucky, paid for my haircut, left what little tip I could spare, and then headed outside.

Wild Side Paint and Auto Body Shop sat opposite Nirvana, on the other side of Main Street. A cat's silhouette stretched beside the bold purple letters outlined with glittering bling.

I gave myself a pep talk before entering, walking the sidewalk in front of Jada's shop and telling myself Taylor had no reason to hold shit against me three years later. He had the life a man could dream about, and I was just a scrub he'd once tossed behind bars.

Ten minutes passed before I had the courage to cross the street and enter the lobby. My former boss's

old store wasn't recognizable anymore. Taylor had
built an actual storefront and tiled the floors, giving the
shop a more reputable look than the original dusty
shack and rusty cash register.

"Sup, man. You need anything?" some kid called to
me from behind the register.

Everyone's attention flew to me. I winced. "I just
wanted to speak with the owner. Is he around?"

"Tay? Yeah. Lemme page him to the front." The guy
leaned away and hit a button. "Taylor, a client needs to
see you in the lobby."

Client. Heh. The kid made me sound all respectable
when I was anything but.

The boss appeared moments later, unchanged from
the man I knew three years ago. He was a broad-
shouldered black guy with pale blue eyes, a cougar
shifter, and Army veteran. With his hair trimmed short
and freshly faded, he looked like he belonged on the
cover of *GQ* in a suit and tie. Or in a Tyler Perry
movie.

He eyed me from across the floor where he wiped
the oil off his hands with a rag. I stood my ground.

"The hell are you doing here?" an aggressive voice
demanded from behind me.

I whirled, coming face-to-face with a big bastard in
blue coveralls sporting the cat emblem on Taylor's sign.
He had a face like a bulldog, arms as big as my thighs,
and a familial resemblance to a teen I'd once given coke
when I was desperate to make some cash.

"I'm just here to see the boss."

"You got a lot of fucking nerve coming around here," the hulking giant said.

"Hey. He's cool," Taylor spoke up. He stepped between us, diffusing the situation with presence alone.

I could tell at a glance, and in a sniff, that he and I were the only shifters in the building.

"Ain't he the—"

"I said he's cool," Taylor repeated, infusing the kind of authority in his voice I only heard from correctional officers in prison and drill sergeants in the movies.

The big guy backed down, and Taylor turned to look me over. His glacier blue eyes studied me, roving over me from head to toe and back again, as if he could peer inside my soul and see my deepest thoughts.

Hell, maybe he could. Some shifters had extra special gifts.

"Come on back to the office, Lyle."

The hard stares continued until we were safe behind the door in complete privacy. I soaked up cool air from the vent over my head and sighed in relief.

All signs of Tito had been erased, even his smell. The old pimp den was gone, replaced by a respectable office with a wooden desk buffed to a glossy sheen. I only smelled motor oil, cat, and a scented candle burning on a nearby file cabinet.

"I guess this isn't a social visit. Water?" When Taylor looked at me, his features lacked judgment and conde-scension. He offered a bottle from a mini fridge behind his desk.

If I was any hotter, I would have poured it over my head. Instead, I twisted off the top and guzzled it down to the last drop.

Taylor laughed. "Long walk here, huh?"

"Yeah…" I wiped my mouth with one wrist, glanced away from him, and cleared my throat. "Look, I'm just going to come right out and say it, man. I need a job. This is what I know, all I know, and right now I don't have a lot of legal options to return to if I wanna make a living." I waved my arm stump.

"How's your arm feeling, by the way?" he asked instead of giving me an answer.

"Like it ain't there," I replied. "Usually."

"Saw you out in your yard the other afternoon. You were getting along pretty well."

I scuffed the toe of my sneaker against the tile floor. "Yeah, better than I expected, I guess. My mom wanted me to try it."

"She why you want this job?"

"Honestly? I know she can't afford to keep me around there forever, and I'm sick of feeling sorry for myself."

"Fair enough. So, what are you looking to do?"

"Whatever you'll give me. Hell, I'll push the damn shop broom around if it means I can earn back the chance to help with the cars."

"There's some changes to the place," Taylor warned.

"I figured as much."

"No drinking. No smoking. You do that shit on your own time, not on mine."

I grimaced. No beers was fine, but going a full day without a ciggie would blow. It didn't take long to get hooked again after my release.

"Sounds good," I agreed. "Anything else?"

"Yeah. I provide you with three sets of coveralls for work. We have a washer here for them, too, so you don't need to worry about taking them home."

"Does this mean I have the job?"

"You can start tomorrow. We open at eight, so I want you here at seven to fill out paperwork. That gonna be a problem?"

I shook my head. "No. No problem at all."

Working in Taylor's shop wasn't so bad once he laid down the law and let the guys know I was part of the team. He made it clear up front there was no room for hazing and bullshit, and that if they couldn't respect his choices, they could walk out the door on their own before he tossed them through it.

Only one guy left, and according to the rest of the guys, it was no big loss. T-Bone, the guy with a face like an English bulldog, told me he'd cripple the rest of my body if he caught me selling even a single loose cigarette.

Since Taylor started me off behind the sales counter, I made the best of it and learned to operate the register with one hand. I rang up customers when it was time to pay for their work, and convinced them to purchase floor mats, air fresheners, and seat covers among other odds and ends.

I smelled Taylor behind me before he said anything. The cat waited for me to notice him, standing in the doorway of his office, arms crossed over his chest. When a few awkward minutes passed, he spoke up first.

"You're not bad at that."

"Not bad at what? Hitting buttons on the register?"

"Nah. Selling to people, especially the ones not in a mood to listen. You could probably sell holy water to an atheist."

"Yeah, well, you know how it is. Had to be a fast talker in my old line of work."

"True, but it's more than that. You've got charisma, when you aren't hating the world."

"I don't hate the world," I muttered.

"Yeah. Sure you don't." Taylor chuckled and rubbed the back of his neck. "Anyway, I just wanted to say keep up the good work."

I blinked. "Thanks."

As business wound down at the end of a Friday night, I was one of the last guys left in the shop, holding on to the keys belonging to the cars they worked on. At a quarter to five, they were pushing it close.

"Sorry, man. Looks like T-Bone overbooked today," one of the mechanics said. "We're working as fast as we can."

Whatever enmity he had against me had faded to a

cordial understanding. I understood that he would beat the living daylights out of me if I stepped out of line. He'd have to take a number. Everyone wanted a piece of my ass if I screwed up.

I shrugged it off. "I get paid by the hour."

The fortune of an overbooked shop earned me an additional hour of overtime. At the fair wage Taylor was paying me, I'd be able to pay Mama's electric bill and even fill her fridge with groceries. Those thoughts bounced through my mind while I followed the sidewalk winding through town, almost oblivious to the late August summer bearing down on my shoulders.

Sheriff Ian MacArthur's SUV rolled up to the curb and kept pace with my stride.

"Hop in. I'll give you a ride."

"Don't need your charity, bird-man," I muttered to the eagle shifter.

"It's over a hundred degrees out," Ian called through the window. "Hottest day of the month according to the weather station."

"Yeah? So?"

"So if you pass out dead on the road, that's more work for me. Reports for me to file. Hell, I might even miss dinner with the wife and kid."

Damn him for making sense. "I didn't plan to walk the entire way on foot. Least not these feet."

"Then let me save you the hassle of carrying your clothes home. C'mon. I don't bite." He winced the moment the words left his mouth. "Sorry."

Against common sense and every lick of good judgment I had, I got in the vehicle. A few minutes in the sun had poured sweat down my brow, stinging my eyes.

Uncomfortable silence filled the first part of the drive. What did I say to the man who had a hand in busting my former boss and seeing me off to jail?

"I talked to your mother once when you were away."

"Away," I repeated dryly.

Ian carried on, ignoring me. "The funny thing about mothers is that they have a habit of remembering the best and omitting the worst. She only had great things to say about her son. Said you gave her money when she ran short, kept her car running, bought her groceries. Could have had your pick of any college, but you stayed back in Quickdraw to take care of her."

I grunted. "College is overrated."

"But since I know you, I was ready to disregard that until I poked deeper. Asked around. Found some old teachers with some interesting stories about you."

I said nothing.

Ian looked over at me. "You wanted to be a veterinarian once and could have been one if you'd enrolled in school and moved away."

"Why does it matter to you?"

"Son, you're not an idiot. Your mother kept every acceptance letter, so why didn't you enroll in A&M and get out of here? I hate to say anything negative about Quickdraw, but this place was crap back then. Even I realize it. Hell, *my* grandfather founded this town, but it's seen its fair share of ups and downs over the years," Ian said.

My back stiffened. What my mama kept and what school I didn't go to was none of MacArthur's business.

He carried on, oblivious to my discomfort. "So I'm curious. What makes a guy like you turn away from education and a solid career to sell drugs in an automotive shop?"

"I like cars."

"Right. Still, though, why here? You could have gone for an engineering degree."

"I didn't want to," I bit out. "We're not all rich boys like you with a free ride to college. My grades were good but not scholarship good."

Ian's unrelenting stare continued, unimpressed with my embittered remarks. "My free ride came by way of the United States government, Lyle. I killed and risked my life for it, doing what's right so you can have the privilege of squandering what your mama's done for you. Now you can cut the lip and listen to me, or you can go back to scowling on the sidewalk like the world owes you something."

"What the fuck do you want from me, old man? I have a job, I come to work every day, I don't steal shit or cause trouble."

"I want you to give something back to the community to make up for the years you preyed on it peddling crack and meth. I want you to meet boys and girls headed the wrong way, so they can talk to someone who's walked their paths. They don't want to listen to me. I'm the rich guy."

"You're the law, sheriff," I muttered.

"Yeah. I don't have anything in common with them, but *you* do."

"Are you for real? You want me to talk to a bunch of kids?" I barked out a harsh laugh. "Man, you gotta be desperate if you're asking me for help."

Ian pulled over down the street from my house, which I appreciated. Last thing I wanted was for Mama to see me getting out of a police car, even if it was from the front.

"You want to hear the entire truth? All right. I *am* desperate. I'm desperate to see these kids change their lives and realize there's another way as long as they work for it and show some dedication." Concern for them added an edge to Ian's soft-spoken voice, and for those moments, he was raw and real, a relatable guy I wanted to hear out.

So I listened.

"There's been a rash of break-ins across town, and I'm worried a couple of them are involved. This is their last shot, and if they screw this up, they'll be on a bus to TYC. "

I stared at him. My criminal mischief didn't begin until adulthood, so I had no experience with the Texas Youth Commission. Most teens on the wrong side of the law knew it as kiddie-prison, a place juveniles served time when probation wouldn't cut it.

"Think about it, Lyle. If you want to change your life and do your mom proud, start showing it."

I considered it. What did I have to lose? Nothing.

But according to Ian, these kids had everything to lose, including the rest of their childhood.

"Sure, why not? Can't fuck 'em up worse than they already are, right?"

2

JULIA

*I*an MacArthur is a great guy and one of my closest friends. He always went above and beyond the call of duty to help others, and because of that, I traveled to Texas to meet a special case.

My memory of the Lone Star State was dry land, dying lawns, and miserable people. It looked like I remembered right.

"Sort of in a heat wave right now," Ian explained from the driver's seat.

I narrowed my eyes at him. "Ugh. Any time you call me to Texas to help you, there's some kind of a drought or unusual flooding."

"You have to be at least a little bit happy to escape the D.C. hustle and bustle."

"At least it's green in Maryland right now," I muttered back. "I can't believe you seriously want me to waste a multi-million dollar prosthetic on a convicted criminal."

"Ex-con," Ian corrected. "Heavy on the ex. But he's about the right build and the appropriate type of shifter for your project. You either shelve it until someone else has the same kind of misfortune, or you put it to use and continue advancing this project. It's up to you."

"Uh-huh." I had an entire file on Lyle Davis, and despite Ian's advocacy in his case, I hadn't been impressed.

"My only request is for you to meet him, and if he fits the bill, you have your man. If not, it only cost you some time and a flight to Texas. And dinner with my family." He beamed proudly.

"What makes you think he won't go back to his old ways?"

"He won't."

"I mean it, Ian. I'm not giving this to some strung out junkie so he can go back to cutting heroine."

"Trust me."

"You always say that."

He peered over at me and grinned. "Have I ever steered you wrong?"

I didn't respond. He always gave exceptional advice.

"Well, you can always wait for some other canine shifter to lose a leg, but we both know you'd be waiting a long time. What are the odds?"

As much as I adored the man, sometimes I wanted to punch him in the face. This was one of those times, but I didn't. Because damn it all to hell, he was right.

I kept my mouth shut for the last leg of the drive.

Quickdraw, Texas was barely a speck on the map, a small town with less than 2000 people.

"You can stay over at our place. We have the room if you don't mind Sophia hounding you."

"I love kids," I assured him. "Charles has…had two."

"I'm sorry about your brother, Jules," Ian replied automatically, as if he'd been waiting for me to bring it up first.

I'd been such a mess at the funeral and practically catatonic at the time. When Ian approached me to pay his respects, I'd lost the last of my courage. I ran away to a nearby restroom and sobbed until I eventually snuck away and took a cab home.

Finding Charles like that in his car… It broke something in me. I didn't think I'd ever move on without my twin, and living without him was like missing part of my soul.

I tried to smile but only grimaced and blinked back tears instead.

"He'll always be missed, not just for the things he did for our squad, but for the friend he was to all of us."

"I know. Thank you, Ian."

My brother had been looking forward to taking over an open spot in Ian's special operative team since Russ, their big bear shifter weapon specialist, had retired to become a full-time family man. One month before his scheduled return to the States, Charles lost part of his left arm and damaged a leg while protecting another soldier from a roadside IED. He'd smelled it too late.

Two months ago, he lost his life after a bout of
depression so bleak nothing would bring him around
again. He'd felt like a burden to his family, and to me,
claiming I'd have more of a life if I wasn't throwing my
every waking minute into building him a replacement.

God, I missed him, and I'd promised myself I would
find someone able to wear this prosthetic arm in his
honor. Could I really turn it over to a junkie?

Ex-junkie, I told myself, trying to be fair.

We pulled up in the last place I expected, outside
the Boys and Girls Club. Ian offered no explanations, a
habit I hadn't missed over the past few years.

"Are you going to tell me anything at all, or do I get
to walk into this blind?"

"Okay, okay. These kids are in the juvenile probation system, so I worked this out between their officer
and parents. Once a week, they come here after the
usual kids are gone. They talk it out with each other
and Lyle for an hour, and we credit them four hours
community service a month for that."

Once Ian parked, we made our way inside past the
front office and into a classroom.

I'd expected Lyle to look like the picture in his file,
overweight and flabby. The reality was a young man in
a close-fitting T-shirt, the sleeves stretched over strong
biceps. His left arm ended about one or two inches
below the elbow, tapered to a neat stump.

Just like Charles. Ian was right; at first sight, their
injuries appeared to be a perfect match.

Blinking rapidly to suppress the emotion stirred by

Lyle's appearance, I leaned against the wall behind one of the eleven kids attending the talk. Their interested eyes glanced over Ian and me, then forgot we were there.

With my arms crossed over my chest, I watched in silence as the air conditioning current blew my hair around my face. Lyle was almost painfully handsome, with a straight, Grecian nose beneath hooded brown eyes and full, firm lips—but he was also my future patient if Ian had anything to say about it.

Why'd he have to be attractive?

Why'd he have to be a former drug addict?

Why'd he have to be so damned built and muscled? He must have spent all three years of his incarceration learning to do one-armed pushups. And pullups. Sweet lord.

I wanted to despise him on principle for appealing to my most basic, animal instinct—you know, the part of me that wanted to shoo Ian and every kid outside to tear his clothes off for a round of hot and dirty, bestial sex on the floor.

The intensity of my daydream took me by surprise. I swallowed and shoved the fantasy aside to focus on reality, all the while wondering what the hell just happened to me.

"Do you regret working for Tito?" a scrawny black kid asked. He had gray eyes, and the fair, medium-brown skin that alluded to a biracial heritage.

"Do I regret it, Kev? Yeah. Sometimes," Lyle said to his group of teens. "I regret it a lot, but guess what?

Regret won't change the things I did. It's done and over with. I can't do anything but do better with my future now. It's okay to make mistakes. We all do it sometimes, but what matters is picking up and learning from it. Being clean three years now gives me a lot of perspective."

Another boy leaned forward in his seat, freckled and strawberry blond with big blue eyes. "So you got your job back at TJ's, but what about your old friends? Don't you miss 'em?"

"They weren't real friends, Jason. I know it's hard to believe it, but the guys you were with that day aren't your pals either. Real friends wouldn't want you to risk your safety for laughs. You're worth more than that."

Ian whispered in my ear, "Just talk with him, Julia. Everyone deserves a second chance, don't you think?"

"Not everyone," I muttered under my breath, earning his sympathetic glance.

Ian knew all about my ex-fiancé, the one I'd walked in on three years ago with some intern in his office—the day before our wedding.

"Fine. Not everyone," he agreed, "but give this guy a chance, will you?"

Their support group wound down and ended, the kids all filing out a couple at a time. Three hung around to ask Lyle a couple questions about doing time, then they left, too, and we were alone with the dog shifter on the other side of the room. I followed Ian over without moving too close. Courtesy among our kind dictated I wait.

Lyle's distrustful brown eyes darted from Ian to me and back again. "Whatcha need, sheriff?"

"I have someone I'd like you to meet. This is Dr. Julia Bearheart. She's the head researcher of a big program out in D.C., and she came down all this way to talk to you about prosthetics."

"Yeah?" His eyes narrowed. "No thanks. Can't afford that stuff."

Lyle kept his distance. I smelled the dog on him at once, the musky underlying scent that was intertwined in all our souls. We all had a little of the beast imprinted on our human bodies, but sometimes it took a good nose to smell it.

Stop breathing it in. Stop, I chided myself, though when I looked up at Lyle again, his nostrils flared and his gaze intensified.

"It's a prototype," I said. "It actually won't cost you a thing beyond your time and cooperation. Some tests and reviews. Allowing me to work on it and perfect the model."

"I'll pass. Whatever this guy told you," he said with a nod toward Ian, "forget it and ignore him."

I clenched my jaw and cast aside the instant attraction to his physical qualities. Bristling, I straightened my back and met Lyle's gaze head-on, undeterred by his bullshit.

"Wow," I spoke up in a droll voice after forcing a dry, brittle laugh. "You dragged me all the way down here to talk to a coward, Ian? You neglected to mention that bit in his history."

"What the fuck?" Lyle's gaze darted from me to Ian's stern features. "I'm not a coward, not that my history is any of your goddamned business."

"Yeah, well, I'm not convin—"

"Hey. *Hey.* Dial it back a bit. Both of you," Ian spoke in his quiet, yet compelling voice.

He was old enough to be my father, his face youthful despite his silver hair and close-trimmed beard. His voice was like magic, having the desired effect of silencing Lyle. And me.

In a softer voice, I said, "You promised a candidate, but this guy doesn't know a damn thing about this, and he's obviously unwilling. I'm not going to waste my time if he wants nothing to do with it. You should have spoken with him first."

"I'm telling you, we do have a candidate for your program," Ian insisted.

"What program?" Lyle's brows raised, and I knew I had him hooked.

"You used to have more patience than this, Jules," Ian said in a low murmur for my ears alone. "Sell the idea to him. Nicely."

Leave it to the eagle to be the wise one. Damn. He saw right through me, but at least he didn't understand my reasons for wanting to put as many miles between myself and Lyle as I could. Beneath the scent of cigarettes and the musk of man, there was something tickling the back of my senses. Something unfamiliar I didn't want to identify.

Sighing, I pushed away from the wall and took a

single step closer to my promised subject. "We're offering you a new arm, and not only for your human guise, but your shifter body as well. No more running around on three legs. You'll receive full functionality again."

Lyle stood straighter. "Is this for real? You're trying to give me something? No cost?"

"No cost, but it's going to mean work—hard work—and lots of dedicated rehab time."

"You trying to say I can't do hard work?"

"Did I say that? I'm telling you what I tell any prosthetic recipient. It's not as easy as strapping on a replacement limb and letting you loose on the world. There are going to be days when it hurts. Days when it feels like you want to give up. I'm just letting you know up front."

Anger flushed a wave of hot color across Lyle's skin, and his jaw clenched, grinding his teeth. "I'll do it."

I had a feeling it had nothing to do with wanting the arm and everything to do with my unvoiced challenge. He knew I didn't think he could do it.

"Excellent," Ian said. "I can see you two are going to become close friends." The sarcasm dripped heavily from his voice.

For one moment, Lyle and I both seemed to be of the same mind. Each of us eyed the sheriff as if we were considering whether punching him would be worth the hassle.

Maybe this guy would work out after all.

And maybe if he remained as much of an ass as first

impressions dictated, it'd be easier to deny the physical attraction my body demanded for me to notice.

"When you get off work tomorrow," I said, offering out a business card, "come by the clinic on Main Street. I've been given an office and exam room there."

"Fine," Lyle snapped back. "I'll be there at six after I lock up."

"Good." I offered a small, tight smile. "Please bring your work schedule for the month, if you can. We'll work out times to fit around your hours as much as possible."

"Fine. Now if you'll excuse me, I gotta go."

Watching him leave, I shook my head and turned to Ian. "He's not going to be easy to work with. Something tells me he doesn't feel like he deserves a new limb, and there's not a damn thing I can do to help him if his heart isn't in it. You know that."

"He's been through a hell of his own," Ian agreed, "but I'm not here to judge him anymore for that shit. The boy served his time." The eagle shifter stroked his chin thoughtfully and gazed at his phone display. "Give Taylor a call tonight, and he'll arrange the schedule as needed. Lyle's too proud to ask for it himself."

I rolled my eyes and nudged a hip into him. "I said I'd work with his schedule, and I meant it. Let him work, I won't take that away from him."

"He puts in long hours, sweetheart. He's going to be burning the wick at both ends and suffering for it if he doesn't cut back a little from these twelve-hour days to work with you. Anyway, Taylor's willing to make him leave on time from now on."

"Fine, fine. I'll talk to Taylor tonight at dinner, if he and his wife are still coming over."

"That's the plan."

"And Betty invited me over for tea tomorrow afternoon." I looked at my former colleague, grinned, and poked him in the side. "I gotta say, I'm glad to see your grandma still bossing you around the place."

He groaned. "Yeah. She says she's going to become immortal only to keep picking at me. And I believe it."

"Cherish every minute."

"I always do."

*D*octor Julia Bearheart had to be the most beautiful woman I'd ever seen. At first I noticed the stink of bird in the air after she and Ian entered, but something unfamiliar and undeniably tempting lingered beneath the scent of eagle. I saw her immediately, and from that moment, I knew I needed to get away from her.

Julia was one of those flawless women who could have modeled to pass time. A few strands of pin-straight hair framed her high cheek bones, the rest drawn into a single neat braid. Even from a distance, I smelled her coyote half.

All I had wanted was to rip her clothes off and kiss her, in no order, and I'd been prepared to storm out to avoid it until she pressed my buttons.

Calling me a coward? I was a lot of things, but a coward would never be one of them.

Didn't she know I had fought an alligator to save

my boss's life? Maybe it wasn't one of the smartest things I'd ever done, but it was the thought that counted, right?

With a scowl firmly etched on my face, I made it to the next corner where I waited for the light to change to the pedestrian symbol. Once I'd hurried across the street, a red pickup truck pulled beside me, and the front passenger window rolled down. Kevin, one of the boys from our meeting, waved at me from the seat.

"Hey, Lyle! You want a ride?"

"I don't—"

"Mom says it's okay. Right, Mom?"

Mrs. Wilson leaned forward to be seen behind the steering wheel, a slightly overweight woman with uneven front teeth in a friendly smile. She wore large aviator shades too big for her oval face. "C'mon in."

I slipped into the rear cab and tilted my face toward the AC vent to soak up the frosty current. "Thanks," I murmured.

"Don't mention it. Chestnut Street, right? We'll drop you off along the way."

They lived about five miles past my house down a long farm road on the outskirts of Quickdraw.

"Yes, ma'am."

"You can call me Hillary. I appreciate the time you've been spending with Kev. Especially after what he—"

"Mom," Kevin groaned.

Chuckling at the mother and son interaction, I relaxed enough to grin at them. "He's a good kid with some awesome skills on the court. I could probably learn a few tricks from him."

Hillary beamed, the model example of an encouraging, supportive mother despite her son's brush with the criminal justice system. "I keep telling him he should go out for the school team."

Kevin sank deeper in his seat and sulked out the window. His mom offered casual conversation until we pulled up outside my house.

"Thanks again for the ride."

"Anytime." Hillary waved.

"See you tomorrow, Lyle," Kevin said.

The aroma of southern comfort food greeted me when I stepped inside our house. Mama waved from the kitchen where she idled in front of the oven with the walker she used on bad days. Years of working two jobs to raise me alone had taken their toll on her joints, producing a degenerated knee and two slipped discs. Mama struggled to get out of bed most days.

But she always had dinner ready for me when I returned from work.

"How's it goin', Ma?"

"Just great. You go ahead and get washed up for dinner. I'm almost finished."

I kissed her cheek then ambled into the bathroom to shower and change into a clean T-shirt and pajama bottoms. By the time I emerged, she'd set the table for us, serving up smothered pepper steak, rolls, and mashed potatoes with gravy.

"It looks delicious."

"You go on ahead and dig in, baby. Tell me about your day."

At first, I hesitated because I didn't want to get her hopes up. Sometimes I thought my lost arm hurt Mama more than it troubled *me*. "Sheriff MacArthur brought some friend of his to town to meet me today."

"Oh? I like Sheriff MacArthur. He's such a nice young man."

"Y'all are almost the same age," I reminded her.

"Easy to forget. Your people stay young so doggone long, I wouldn't think him to be in his fifties even with all that white hair." She sighed, and this wistful look came over her face, the dreamy-eyed gaze she always had whenever she remembered my no-good daddy.

I wished I could remember him sometimes, but I didn't begrudge her the good memories she kept of the absent figure from our lives. He must have had some good qualities about him for Mama to fall to completely and absolutely in love and still pine for him almost twenty-eight years later.

"So what did the sheriff and his friend want?"

"They came to make me an offer about some kind of government program. If I do it, I get an arm."

She blinked. "A what?"

At least it sounded as crazy to her as it did to me. I chuckled wryly and sat at the dinner table. "An arm, Mama. They wanna give me a new arm, one like those prosthetics we saw on the news."

Mama sat with me in the next chair, the dishrag still in her hands. "Really? What's it going to cost?"

"Nothing, or so they claim. I get to head over to this doctor's office tomorrow and talk with her all about it."

Mama's blue eyes lit up with glee, but as soon as she opened her mouth to speak, she quieted again and deep wrinkles creased between her graying brows. "How do you feel about it?"

"Honestly? I don't know. I wanna be excited, but it feels too good to be true, like somebody's gonna bust out and say the joke's all on me the moment I let my guard down."

She pursed her lips. "Do you want me to come with you to see this doctor?"

"No, no. I'm going to head over and see her after work."

Common sense told me I should invite my mother along to keep me honest. Then I remembered I didn't have a chance in hell with Julia Bearheart, so it didn't matter if I went alone or not. She was so far out of my league I'd need a spaceship to reach her.

Fate and bad decisions had already taken my arm, but I didn't think it was cruel enough to put the perfect woman in front of me, at a time in my life when she was absolutely unobtainable.

After all, what the hell would a doctor want with an ex-junkie?

That question troubled me all night long, making me toss and turn in bed while memories of her cocoa brown eyes—so dark they could be black—beckoned me like some siren's call. I couldn't get her off of my mind.

By sunrise, I'd barely slept a wink. Mama must have heard my restless wandering through the house because I awakened to a pot of black coffee and a heavy breakfast of eggs, bacon, and toast with homemade peach preserves. I guzzled the coffee down, ate, and stood like a zombie in the shower until I regained enough life in my bones to make the trek to town on foot.

The Webbers waved to me in passing from their seats on the porch swing. Startled, I almost didn't remember to wave back. The older couple, a man in his seventies and his equally white-haired wife, lived at the end of the lane where our street met the farm road. A big fence surrounded their property, and about five dogs ran wild inside it. They'd had dogs for as long as I could remember, friendly creatures of all breeds and sizes from border collies to a massive Dane.

The dogs leapt at the fence and scratched at it, eager to see me. Normal canines recognized me as a shifter, and either lost their shit to escape my presence or went out of their way to be friends. These guys, panting and whining for attention, wanted the latter.

I grinned and lingered long enough to pet the poodle standing on her hind legs for attention.

"How's that mother of yours, Lyle? Haven't seen Peggy in a while," Mrs. Webber called.

"Mama's doing better than usual. She came outside to fetch the eggs this morning." I stood at their fence for a while to chat.

"I sure would like if she'd come visit us soon. You'll tell her, won't you, baby?"

"Sure will, Mrs. Webber."

I waved goodbye and continued down the road, and as usual, Taylor arrived about fifteen minutes after me to open up.

"How long you been sitting out here?" he asked me, raising his brows.

"Not long," I assured him.

"Hm."

He didn't say anything else as he let me inside. We each had our own routine, and my morning duties involved clicking on the lights and opening the blinds while he went to the back to deactivate the alarm system. I powered on the register, opened the shutters, and raised the doors to the garage.

Then I made coffee because Luis and T-Bone lived on Maxwell House.

"Taylor. You got a moment, man?"

"Sure, dawg, what's up?"

"It's, uh, kinda personal."

Taylor gestured toward his open office, urging me ahead of him and inside to a seat. I sat down, and he crossed behind the desk to sit opposite me.

"What's on your mind?"

Thinking about Julia made my palms sweaty. "Mac-Arthur brought a friend, and I was wondering if you know her, too."

"Julia? Yeah. Good friend to everyone, you could

say. She used to fill in for Sasha on the team whenever we needed a medic."

"Tell me about her," I blurted out.

His brows shot up, then a slow grin came over his face. "I'll tell you everything I can that's not personal or classified if you'll tell me why you're asking."

"She's offering me a new forearm, and if she's going to be messing with this," I said while waving my left arm at him, "I want to know what kind of person she is."

He leaned back in his seat and raised a mug of coffee to his lips. "Shit... Where to start, then. Julia's more than a friend—another little sister to us, you could say."

My heart sank a little. Baby sister to a group of some of the toughest men I knew. Men with every reason to dislike me, despite Taylor and Ian's recent acceptance. It was one more reason to keep well away from the coyote.

"She a good doctor?"

"She's brilliant and was always designing these inventions, until one day, the blueprints for one of them wound up on the desk of some bigwig way above my pay grade. I think Ian did it. He won't own up to it, but it earned her a one-way ticket out of the service and into a sweet civilian gig leading her own research department.

"So she's a super genius."

"Pretty much." Taylor chuckled.

"Tony Stark level genius." Enough of a genius to

know I wasn't worth shit to her beyond being her guinea pig.

"Yup."

"Christ," I groaned before drowning my disappointment in my cup.

Taylor smiled at me, oblivious to my dilemma. "That soothe your worries some?"

"Yeah. S'pose it does."

The truth cut like a double-sided blade. On one hand, I'd hoped to have even a sliver of a chance, but on the other, I knew better and didn't think I was worth her trouble. With my hopes dashed, I felt only a bleak, hollow hole where my optimism had once resided.

At least there was the promise of a new arm.

"If she's giving you a new arm..." Taylor pursed his lips and studied me with a sudden intensity. "Give it a fair shot. Shifters are her area of expertise, if you get my meaning. You won't get another offer like this if you turn it down, so just think it over real good. Take a day or two if you have to. She won't rush you."

"I will, thanks."

The bell above the lobby's door chimed, alerting me to the arrival of a customer. I hustled out to the store counter and put on my service-with-a-smile attitude.

Eight hours. Eight more hours until I could see her again. Maybe I couldn't have her, but I could damned sure enjoy looking at her.

JULIA

*L*ife had a funny way of tossing curveballs when they weren't expected. Fate took something away and it didn't always give back, but I hadn't yet determined what I'd done to deserve the latest sadistic twist to my screwed up life.

First I'd lost Charles, then my sister-in-law became a control freak about their kids, and now... instantaneous shifter attraction to an ex-con.

"Dr. Bearheart, Mr. Davis is here to see you."

My pulse picked up like I had finished a marathon.

Controlling my expression, I looked up from my computer screen to the friendly young nurse and smiled. "Thanks, Lillian. Send him back, would you?"

Get a grip on yourself. I had about thirty seconds to prepare. The scent of dog drifted down the hall through my open door. Dog and Marlboros. I tried to focus on the latter and ground myself in reality, because nothing was more unattractive than the stink of tobacco.

Lyle Davis came from around the corner and lingered in the doorway. I marveled over the difference between him now and the photographs of a chubby, awkward ginger in his mid-twenties. My gaze dipped to his stomach, his abs flat and toned beneath a plain T-shirt. His jeans fit snug, fastened with a thick leather belt with the standard, obnoxious, and huge Lone Star State buckle southerners loved.

I refused to let my attention drift any lower.

Too late. He was probably packing under that ridiculous belt buckle.

"Have a seat," I invited.

The loaned office was small but tidy, a fraction of the workspace given to me in D.C. after I left the navy. I had air, a desk, a filing cabinet, and all the essentials.

Lyle studied me as he moved to the cushioned chair across from my desk, and I imagined a dog with his hackles raised, slinking over while eyeing a potential threat.

"Today we'll just go over the formalities. I have some papers for you to look over and sign." I handed him a clipboard with a thick stack clipped to it. "Feel free to take them home, or even have a lawyer look at them if you like. It's up to you. The non-disclosure agreement is the top form there."

"Don't have a lawyer," he replied. With a little dexterity, he removed the cap from the pen with one hand then scrawled his name across the top without questioning the form. "Won't nobody hear anything about it from me."

"Then take it all home, look it over, and we'll go from there. You already have my card, so feel free to call at any time with questions." I leaned over and took the NDA, leaving him with the rest.

"MacArthur mentioned a little about it and said it's some super top secret spy shit like *Agents of Shield*."

"That's one way to put it." Leave it to Ian to use a geektastic television show as an analogy. "We've been working with some new polymers and technology to make a prosthetic that will shift with you." I waited, giving him a chance to let that soak in.

He studied me in silence, his brown eyes narrowed in suspicion. He glanced around the room and discreetly sniffed the air, nostrils flaring despite his effort to be lowkey. He didn't trust it, or me. "I can run again on four legs? How much is this gonna cost?"

"As I said before, there will be no cost. This is a prototype, and you'll be, well, our test subject for lack of a better term. You will be the first recipient of such a device. *Ever.* Consider it to be a clinical trial where I'm allowed to study you for a two-year term, and in return, you get to keep the device. All medical appointments in regards to the prosthetic are also covered. Any medications prescribed, covered."

"A clinical trial," Lyle repeated. He shuffled the stack of papers against his jean clad thigh, the denim tight enough to showcase the developed muscle beneath.

I tore my gaze back to his quizzical
expression. "Yes."

"What's it going to do to me?" he asked. "Is there a
surgical procedure involved? If the risks outweigh the
benefits, will I be able to have it removed at any time?
This isn't just a prosthetic, is it? I've been reading stuff
about brain-controlled bionic limbs. What's the testing
period? This is all inside the book of papers, isn't it?"
He blurted out one question after the next, and the
redneck facade vanished to reveal the intelligent individual beneath his tough-guy veneer.

Ian was right. He wasn't an idiot after all.

I'd misjudged the guy. The questions impressed me,
and showed that he'd taken some time to do some
cursory research.

"Yes, the answer to every question is inside that
packet, but I'm happy to answer any questions you
have while we're here face-to-face. As for the limb, it'll
restore complete mobility to you in both forms, hopefully without pain. If you experience phantom limb
sensations, those will vanish. And yes, there is surgery
involved. Is that going to be all right?"

Some of the distrust faded. "What kind of surgery?"

"This isn't your typical prosthetic. It's meant to be a
limb replacement, Mr. Davis, meaning it's going to
become a permanent part of your body. It will be fused
to your radial bone and ulna. It's also my hope to give
you some sensation back, in a manner of speaking." I
cleared my throat and took a sip from a nearby mug of
tepid coffee before continuing. "Regarding the possi-

bility of removal, it won't be easy and shouldn't be
done unless there's extreme pain or a danger to your
well-being. As for the risks, there is always a risk
whenever surgery is involved. Infection may occur,
creating inflammation and cellular necrosis at the site."

"Okay. Why me though? I mean, there's gotta be
more people around better for this."

While pursing my lips in thought, I studied him and
tapped my fingers against the desktop. "Each prosthetic is designed to fit its intended recipient," I began
in a slow, controlled voice. "These aren't mass
produced, nor will they ever be. Not only does the limb
have to fit your human shape, it has to be designed for
your animal as well. This particular one was meant for
a coyote. Not exactly a coonhound, I know, but your
sizes are close enough of a match that I'm confident
this limb will work for you with some minor
adjustments."

"That's a big assumption to make. You've never
seen me."

"I have medical files from your…incarceration."
Because of his unique abilities, he'd been examined
before and after transformation, in the off chance he
tried to escape using his dog form.

In the photograph, his body had a handsome coat to
match his red hair, but he hadn't been a good example
of canine fitness. I'd put money on betting that had
changed, because the human in front of me didn't
match the man photographed when the prison officials
documented his tattoos.

Prison had changed Lyle for the better. He wasn't a huge guy like Russ, or as muscled as Taylor, but closer in size to Ian with a lean swimmer's physique.

"Oh." His expression closed off again.

"You're about eighty-five pounds, give or take, and about this tall," I estimated, holding my hand about thirty inches from the ground.

He blinked at me.

"I've been doing this for a while. Shapeshifter sizes are always a little larger than a typical animal, but still proportionate."

"So what happened, then? Why isn't that coyote getting his arm?"

Expecting the question didn't stop the surge of raw grief. My throat tightened, and I looked away to stab the laptop keyboard with my fingers, feigning interest in the screen. Anything to disguise my emotions for the moment.

"He died," I answered, short and clipped.

Lyle studied me, his eyes appearing more intense and intelligent by the minute.

Shaken by becoming the one under close observation, I cleared my throat. "Anyway, will that be all, Mr. Davis, or do you have more questions?"

"Lyle," he corrected me. "Thanks, I guess. For giving me a chance."

"I'll still need to acquire the exact measurements of the limb in both forms next vis—"

"You ain't gonna do it now?"

"No, not now," I replied. "Go through the paperwork. Read it. Make sure you're going to be okay with everything detailed. Then, when everything official is signed, we'll begin to work. If you'd like to come by the same time tomorrow, great. If you need an extra day, just give me a call, and that will be fine, too."

"All right." He held the stack of forms and papers to his chest and pushed out of the seat, surprisingly graceful for a dog shifter. "Thanks, then. I'll be back tomorrow, Dr. Bearheart."

As I watched him leave, I wondered what the hell Ian had gotten me into this time.

*A*fter sorting through keys, I plucked out a pair with a purple rabbit's foot and passed it to the young woman on the other side of the counter.

"You have a nice afternoon, ma'am," I wished her. She couldn't be more than twenty-five, no younger than sixteen with a body like hers, but for the sake of my stiffening cock, I hoped she was on the legal side of that range.

Her green eyes twinkled as she smiled back at me. "You, too, sir," she replied before her gaze dropped down to my missing limb. An unspoken question hung on her lips, but she didn't ask.

I could read it just the same.

She was gone and out the door before T-Bone whistled. "Man, that was one fine girl. Great ass. Too bad TJ's got rules about work and play. You could have had her number."

"You think so?"

"He-eh-ell yeah, man. She practically eye-fucked you."

Not that it mattered, but it made me feel good all the same. Better than the unimpressed, baleful glares the doc occasionally gave me. I had her stack of papers in a manila envelope behind the counter, ready and waiting for when my shift ended. T-bone took over behind the counter when I clocked out, then I headed out into the afternoon heat on foot to the clinic.

God it was hot. The heat shimmered off the pavement in waves. I couldn't wait for fall to actually kick in and the cool weather to arrive. Late summers sucked.

With only a couple blocks between the shop and our town's only medical clinic, I'd be at her office with time to spare. Or would have been, if I didn't spy a trio of young men standing in the shade of the florist's red overhang. I didn't recognize one of them, but two of the boys stood out as kids I mentored for Ian. My kids.

"Man, why you gotta be such a pussy? Just take one," the unfamiliar teen demanded. He leaned forward, postured aggressively toward the others.

"I don't know… My mom might piss test me again," Kevin muttered. "Look, I don't—"

"Hey, y'all!" I called out. Deciding to feign ignorance, I jogged toward them, and the three turned their terrified faces toward me. Their eyes grew large and panicked like I was an actual authority figure with some ability to punish them.

Kevin immediately became relieved. "Hi, Lyle." He fist-bumped me.

"Sup, man," Brett said, offering a hand.

I clasped my right with his and grinned. "What y'all doin'?"

The third kid glanced away and kept his hands in his pockets. Brett and Kevin were good kids in shitty home situations, but this third kid made me want to beat his ass on principle. He was closer to adulthood than the other two, at least seventeen, with enough facial hair on his chin to compete with me. And he smelled like a drug bust waiting to happen.

"Nothin', man. We were just chattin'," the older teen said, lying through his teeth since he didn't know I could smell the pills in his pocket.

"Sweet, then it won't hurt nothin' if I borrow these two. We need to discuss some important crap before our next meeting, right?"

Before the boys could protest, I pressed what remained of my left arm against Brett's back and guided Kevin away with my right around his shoulders. I didn't stop until we were down the street past the post office and I was sure their bully friend wasn't following.

"You two good?"

"Yeah. Smooth save," Brett admitted.

"He hassle you guys a lot?"

Kevin ducked his head and shrugged, but Brett spoke up without hesitation. "Yeah, sometimes. He hangs with Eddie and Manuelo."

"Who is he?"

"Some asshole who came from Riverside about a year ago. His name's Jed. Failed his junior year twice so he's stuck with us," Kevin said.

"*We're* stuck with him," Brett grumbled. "He has some friends who aren't in school anymore and sometimes they ride up to pick on the rest of us, but nobody cares because his dad owns that new convenience store and has a ton of money. We can't get away from him."

Considering the strong, earthy smell of prescription medicine lingering around the guy and what I suspected was a pocket of narcotics and benzos—sedatives and hypnotics—I made up my mind to offer the boys any help I could give them. "Any time you need an excuse to get away from him, feel free to use me."

The two boys exchanged glances then nodded at me.

"Thanks, Lyle. Hey, you got time for some hoops?" Brett asked.

"Not today. Gotta go see the doc. You can walk me there then double back on Cherry Lane to avoid your friend."

Along the way, we talked about basketball and our fantasy football picks. The boys and I had made our own league for fun, with no money involved. I had fifty dollars invested in a second league with the guys at the garage. When we reached the clinic, I hung around outside the door and watched Brett and Kevin until they disappeared down the road.

I'd have to say something to Ian. The irony of that

thought wasn't lost on me, and I scoffed at myself as I stepped inside.

A nurse led me into an examination room this time, and I felt the eyes of the other med techs on me. They knew who I was, knew what I'd done, and probably wondered why I was here getting some sort of special treatment. Hell, even the people out in the lobby stared when I was waved through.

Doc Bearheart had on a skirt, one of those tight ones that came down to her knees, and a pair of killer heels with pink leopard spots. Her white lab coat hung over a grey silk blouse, and she wore her black hair in a bun. Two earrings, a pair of barn owl feathers with blue clay beads attached to the metal hooks, dangled from her ears.

How hadn't I noticed those curves before? I'd thought she was scrawny, but she was lithe and shapely at the same time, blessed with this round booty that should have required her to have a license for carrying a lethal weapon. Once I remembered how to walk, I slipped over to the table as directed while she perused the paperwork I'd brought back.

I couldn't focus on what I came for when her mouth was a perfect cupid's bow with just the right amount of gloss. My cock went granite hard, and my mind flew from zero to filthy at Mach speed.

"Everything seems to be in order here. Hand, please." She dismissed the nurse and took my wrist. She didn't delegate the standard assessment shit, taking my pulse and blood pressure herself.

Damn, her hands felt like ice, but I wanted her to touch me anyway.

"Well?" I asked at the end after she removed the cuff.

"One thing we need to discuss is your smoking. If you want this limb, you need to quit."

I groaned. She found the magic words to distract me from imagining my dick in her mouth. "I've been smoking for years."

"Doesn't matter. You'll have to remain healthy during these trials, and you certainly went without them while in prison."

Too late to back out now. I'd already signed over my life to them for the next two years. And in the grand scheme of things, having an arm meant more to me than smoking cigarettes. "Fine."

"Good. I'd prefer not to pollute your body with patches and drugs, so cold turkey is the best way to go, but if you struggle, I'll write a prescription."

"Don't need a patch."

"All right." She gave me a brief, half smile.

It made my stomach do a funny little flop, like I cared about her approval. I did. God, I cared so much about her approval. I'd do backflips for tummy rubs.

"How's my blood pressure? It was kind of high in prison."

"What was it then?"

"I think it was 155 over 90," I tell her. "They were going to put me on some medication, but I got out first."

"Well, that's changed. Your vitals are good. Blood pressure is 110 over 70. Heart rate is slightly elevated but nothing abnormal. If you could take off your shirt for me, please, I'll get some measurements."

Dressing and undressing with one hand took practice, but I unbuttoned the shirt without more than a grumble. Taylor joked about my transformation from pudgy gang enforcer to buff ex-con, but I still had trouble accepting this new body was mine. All flat planes and carved muscle from my chest to my abs, and indents around the hip area that made ladies' legs turn to jello.

Except this lady, apparently. I couldn't even get a damned second glance from her. She pulled a soft measuring tape from her pocket and got to work, having me extend my left arm this way and that, measuring length and circumference from different angles. She didn't even say much beyond recording each number with her smartphone's voice recorder.

"All right, now I'll need to do the same for your hound." She stepped back but didn't leave the room, putting her back to me while she tapped notes into her laptop. "We'll also make a mold of your stump in each form sometime later, but for now I need this data."

"How long before the surgery?" I asked while unfastening my belt.

After wiggling my jeans loose and shucking my shorts down to my ankles, I made a clumsy pile of clothes on the chair. Shifting forms and moving to a lower vantage point treated me to the sight of her perfectly round ass.

I'd never get enough of seeing that.

"Next month, most likely. There are lots of things to consider before we cut you open and make a permanent attachment. We'll fit you first with a normal prosthetic, something to wean you onto the idea. See how you do with a regular one. We'll start that next week. In the meantime, I'll be taking you into Houston for an MRI and some other tests."

I couldn't answer, but I mimicked her stern countenance and dipped my head in a nod.

Everything about her was amplified in my dog form, my sense of smell sharpened by the transformation. A definite hint of coyote lingered on her skin, filling the room with the aroma of young and virile woman.

I suppressed the wild, innate urge to shove my nose against her crotch and glanced down at the white linoleum tiles instead.

What the hell was wrong with me?

"Hop on up." She pushed a chair by the bed and waited for me to get back on the exam table.

It wasn't easy, and I nearly fell off in my scramble to get up. Then she went through the whole process again, taking measurements. She hadn't done much touching beyond what was necessary before, but this time she gave my ears a ruffle and my neck a good deep rub, more at ease.

"I'll have to make some adjustments to the limb, but

I think it will fit. You're a tad more muscular than the sergeant was…"

Those fingers felt so damned good, melting the tension from my shoulders and back until I was almost limp beneath her hands. She knew all the best spots to touch and where to press, nearly distracting me from the first solid hint I'd picked up since our introduction. Someone close to her had died.

Whenever she brought up the original, intended recipient of my future arm, her entire face drooped and the light in her eyes dimmed. Her hard ass act made sense. I wasn't just receiving a piece of her life's work; she and Ian had offered me a gift intended for someone she'd cared about. Suddenly, the matter of my success in her program was less about wanting to prove her wrong and more to do with making her proud.

"That's all I need for today. You're free to change and head home. I'll be in the office next door if you have any questions." She left with her laptop, leaving me to wonder about the dead sergeant's identity.

A lover? Husband? No, she didn't wear a ring or have a pale strip where one should have been.

No shame in looking, right? With the door closed, I shifted back and took my time getting dressed.

Becoming her patient, on top of my criminal history, had firmly put me in the professional contact only zone. Despite that, I paused in the doorway of her office and admired the curve of her high cheek bones, the slim angles of her face. She'd taken down her bun, and dark hair fell over her shoulders in a raven cascade.

"Doc?"

"Yes?" She looked up from the computer screen and gave me her full attention.

"Just wanted to say thanks." A quick glance up and down the hall revealed we were all alone. "I know the odds of finding another dog with the same injury in the same limb were a long shot, but y'all didn't have to choose me. Thanks." And because I wanted her to smile at me just once, I'd tolerate whatever pain and discomfort her testing would throw my way.

"You should thank Ian—Sheriff MacArthur. He submitted your information to me." Her smile was tight. Polite. "Get off the cancer sticks, and I'll schedule your MRI for a week from now. Do you think you can arrange for a day off from work?"

"Sure."

Her smell remained with me during the walk home, unforgettable and impossible to get out of my head. I tossed the box of Marlboros in my pocket in the trash along the way and hoped I had the balls to stick with it this time.

~

The upside of living in a quiet town like Quickdraw was the lack of crime. After Ian and his friends chased Tito and his gang out, this place returned to the idyllic lifestyle of the past.

Or had until recently. I'd just reached Main Street when I noticed Ian's SUV parked in front of the florist beside a QPD white cruiser. He leaned against the vehicle with his arms crossed, in deep discussion with another officer, and I would have been content to hurry by without disturbing them if both didn't wave.

Slowing down, I waved back and decided to poke my nose into police business. "Damn, what happened here?"

The flower shop's door hung loose off the hinges, and the glass inlay was shattered. Mama had always admired that door, saying how fancy it was with the stained glass rose design.

"Someone robbed Mr. George," the officer replied.

"What? Someone decide they had a pressing need for some daisies or something?"

Ian shook his head. "They trashed his register and broke into the cabinet with the crystal vases."

I frowned. I'd busted into my fair share of places during my time with Tito, but we'd never done anything like this.

"It's sloppy," I muttered. "Stuff like that ain't easy to sell, either. Not here at least. Mr. George makes those vases so the thieves would have to go down to Houston. There's nobody within fifty miles who'll take them."

Ian raised a brow. Apparently I'd told him something he didn't know. "Well, thanks. So, ah, let's say I was interested in unloading some goods. Where would I—"

"I'm not telling you that too. Y'all can do some police work and figure that one out."

My bet was that the thief didn't know Mr. George created most of the work inside his shop. He was a master level glassblower, the kind of guy who could make beautiful figurines and animals in a few minutes flat. Every year during the county fair, he'd set up his stall and work magic in front of the crowds.

"So what *will* you tell us?" Officer Winslow asked, skipping right to the chase.

I sighed. "Neither of you heard a thing from me, okay? My guess, it's someone who doesn't know the town. Someone passing through or new to Quickdraw hoping to make some fast money. Anybody with some common sense who's done this before knows a cash register is cleaned out at night. You *might* find some change for the next day, but it's no sure thing, you know?"

"He had seventy bucks beneath the till," Ian said.

"Yeah, not worth the risk. Thief was desperate or ignorant."

Winslow rubbed his chin. "Would you think it was a teen?"

Shit. I'd bet it was a teen. I clammed up again, worried about *my* kids and whether they were involved.

"It's a kid," Ian said softly. "You can tell from his face."

"Goddammit, MacArthur." I spun and moved onto

the curb again to continue toward the garage, aware of Ian hot on my heels.

"No one is gonna go pointing fingers at your group if that's what you were thinking," Ian assured me.

I exhaled a sigh of relief and unclenched my right fist.

"If you could talk to them, though, see if maybe one of them might know something. They're more likely to talk to you than me."

"All right."

"Thanks. Hey. One more thing."

I paused and turned on a heel to look at him, raising my brows. "What?"

"Real proud of how well you've been doing since your release, Lyle. With both the kids and accepting Julia's offer. Thanks for that."

"Yeah, well, seems like I have you to thank for getting her to offer me the arm at all. I'm not so sure she thinks much of me." She'd probably be happier to have a junkyard dog than me to deal with.

Ian scoffed and clapped the back of my shoulder. "Don't let her attitude deter you, son. When it comes to her pet project, she can be very focused. Anyway, don't let me keep you."

Despite initially getting off on the wrong foot with Julia, a warm flush came over me at the thought of having her hands on me again, in either form. Human skin or dog fur, I wanted it, and I'd die before I told MacArthur how I felt about his colleague.

With a wave, I continued down the road on my way

to Taylor's and saw T-Bone opening for the day. He and Taylor alternated the responsibility of opening in the mornings even though T-Bone wasn't much of a morning person.

When I wasn't cashing out auto jobs, I spent most of the shift wondering how I'd approach the burglary subject with the kids, and the rest of the time daydreaming about Julia because she flit through my mind like a ghost at inconvenient moments.

I'd talk to them. Not because Ian asked me to snoop, but because this was my one chance to save them from making my mistakes.

Even if I already knew in my heart none of them would spill it.

6

JULIA

I'd worried about being stuck in the car with
Lyle all morning and preemptively taken a
couple aspirin to ward off a migraine. My sensitive
nose hadn't been able to deal with it before, but he
actually smelled...nice.

Without the tobacco odor masking his natural
scent, I picked up the smell of soap and clean skin, of
snuggly, red-furred dog and attractive man. I'd wanted
to cuddle him so bad that day in the examination room
and rub my cheek against his furry face, but until now,
his bad habit had made it all the more easy to resist
him and maintain a professional demeanor.

I eyed his clean clothes, noticing he'd taken some
effort in his appearance for the day. His jeans were
devoid of the usual oil stains and tears, the T-shirt
looked new, and he'd even scraped the mud from his
boots.

Now I worried about how I'd resist him, trapped in

a car for hours with his tantalizing scent surrounding me.

"Any questions about the procedure today?" I asked as I cranked the engine. Business. I needed to focus on business.

"No," he replied before gazing out the window, a surprisingly quiet passenger in my borrowed car.

Taylor had a couple on hand, projects he built up, maintained, and used for a shuttle service if a customer needed to go home or make a pit stop in Quickdraw while the boys worked on their car. The one loaned to me was a roomy, luxury sedan with the exotic, aromatic oils I'd associate with the Middle East or India. His wife owned this fantastic spa in town that I'd been promising to visit for a pamper package, and she made her own line of natural air fresheners from essential oils for his vehicles.

"Really? What, did you look everything up online?"

He looked insulted. "I know what an MRI does."

"All right then." If he wanted to be that way, fine. I hated driving though. I especially hated long drives, and talking helped keep me awake and pass the time.

I managed to go an hour without forcing more conversation. He remained silent even when I flipped constantly through the channels to find a good song, or I grumbled about crappy drivers who deserved to have their licenses revoked.

"What do you do at Taylor's shop?"

Lyle glanced away from the window for the first time since we left Quickdraw. His brows slid

together, forming deep lines in his brow. An
awkward few seconds passed before he said in a
measured voice, like he was talking to a child. "I clean
up the messes and cash out the customers.
Nothing big."

"Ah." Not a big talker, this guy. After another ten
minutes, I nudged the conversation again. I liked his
voice and the smooth southern drawl. "What do you
want to do after you get the arm?"

"Work on cars. Fix stuff," he mumbled before
tossing his shoulders in a distracted shrug. Something
had changed in the time since our last appointment.
"How long until we're there?"

"Another hour. Maybe two if traffic backs up when
we get into Houston. In a rush?" I looked over again
and frowned. "Did something come up back home?" Or
was he being surly on general principle?

He shook his head.

Since meeting the hound, I'd seen him transition
through a range of emotions from rebellious and self-
pitying to appreciative and almost…sweet. The new,
quieter Lyle unsettled me.

Because I had seen it in my brother before he gave
up. My mouth went dry.

"Not in a rush, ma'am, was only curious about how
far south of Houston we'd have to travel to get to this
place."

"Ma'am," I repeated, unable to help myself. God, I
wasn't *that* much older than him, was I? Only thirty-
seven, certainly not old enough to warrant ma'am.

Though if we were dating, I'd definitely feel like I was robbing the cradle.

"Let's, uh, drop the ma'am, okay? I'm a civilian now, for one, and it makes me feel like a grandma or something. As for how far we're going, the VA hospital is in central Houston, a little on the south side. Are you familiar with the city at all?"

The dense lines in his forehead didn't ease. He shook his head. "You're in Texas now. It's gonna be ma'am most places you go. Anyway, no, I'm not too familiar with central Houston. Only came down this way if we had—" He stopped and looked down at his lap. "Anyway, I don't come down this way often."

I read between the lines. He never came this way unless he had drugs to deal.

"You're more than welcome to call me Julia," I told him in a gentle voice before deciding to probe for information. "So you're particularly quiet today. Is there something on your mind?"

"No."

Well. If he wouldn't talk, I'd do the chatter for both of us, and after a moment, I blurted out, "I hate driving. Like…I really, really hate long drives. It makes me tired. Sad, right?"

After tilting his head back against the headrest, he shook his head and resumed watching the rolling hills of Texas countryside bordering I-45. Occasionally, he fidgeted with the chain connecting the wallet in his jean pocket to his belt loop.

"I miss driving almost as much as I missed running

while I was locked up. I guess I'll be able to do it again one day, right?"

He didn't look at me again, but I enjoyed a wistful moment of studying his profile and admiring the view.

"Lots of people drive one handed, don't they?" I considered it, eyed his arm again, and thought of all the modifications he would need to safely operate a vehicle. How annoying it would be to try and flip the blinker on or turn on the windshield wipers.

Screw that. If I had my way, a few months from now he wouldn't need any of that, and he'd be cruising down the road with two functional hands.

"You're talking to me a lot today," he said after a moment.

"Like I said, I hate driving, and it feels weird to sit in a car with someone and not talk."

"Oh." He said it quietly, barely a quiet murmur of sound, a kicked puppy beside me who had become more melancholy than sulky.

"So...tell me a bit about yourself. Something all those files wouldn't tell me. We can make it an even exchange if you want. You answer my questions, and I'll answer one for you."

"Fine. I had a cat when I was in prison."

It wasn't what I'd expected. "How did you have a cat in prison? I mean, did they keep them as pets, or was it a stray?"

He glanced down at his remaining hand and turned it over palm up, then down again, his brow wrinkled in concentration. "A stray prison cat. There's a lot of them out in the country, and they breed out of control. So anyway, I was eating tuna in the day room one morning, and he came in through a hole in the window. I figured he had to be hungry and shared with him, but he found me outside a few days later on the rec yard and followed me around there, too. We weren't supposed to have pets, but the prisons are so old and busted down they can't really keep animals out everywhere. There were guys with pet rats and all kinds of shit. Turtles. Snakes. I had a cat. Don't tell Taylor."

"And it hung around? Brave cat." I chuckled and flipped through the stations during the commercial break, searching for music to avoid listening to ads. "Being what you are and all, I mean. Cats tend to hiss at me, so I just don't bother with them."

"Yeah. He was. I kinda miss him. He was all black, had this white patch on his chest, so he stood out from the other black cats."

"Sounds pretty. Handsome, I guess. Your turn. To ask a question, I mean."

The tension in his shoulders visibly eased away, diminished by a fraction. He even made eye contact with me again. "What do you do when you aren't doing doctor things?"

"I read a lot. But, uh, I'm guessing that's not what you mean. I like to go hiking and rock climbing, actually. Not a lot of that in the D.C. area, so I settle for the gym climbing wall."

"Climbing is fun," he agreed. "MacArthur's got a lot

of space back on his land for hiking. He tried to invite me last week."

"Just so you know, Ian doesn't do charity cases. I mean, he donates to charity, but he doesn't do things out of pity for someone. If he offered, he meant it. You should take him up on it."

"He's an okay guy," was as much a compliment as he could pay to Ian. Something passed over his expression, a softening and a look of melancholy.

According to his file and what I'd read, Lyle didn't have a father of his own. Ian was old enough to be his.

I pulled over to the right lane when GPS announced my exit was coming up. "Ian says you live with your mom. That a long term plan or just for now while you get on your feet?"

Finally, I was getting somewhere with him, only for him to grunt and his expression to close up. "I had my own place before I was locked up. Anyway, I give her most of my checks. I'm not a freeloader."

"Never said you were. I think it's nice, helping your mom out. She's lucky to have you around to care for her. I…" How much did I share? How much did I want to share? "My folks aren't around anymore. They died a few years ago. Mom had cancer, and Dad followed not too long after from a broken heart. They could never be apart for long, you know?"

His gaze darted back to me, startled. "Yeah. I read about that once. I guess it's common when people are older. More for shifters. Which one was the coyote? Or was it both?"

"Both." I wasn't surprised he'd figured it out. Shifters could sniff out shifters, and unlike certain gargantuan, mythological creatures, coyotes were a common species. "And yeah, they had a really deep connection. True mates. So, it's just me now." Because my brother had given up. Because I'd failed him and didn't realize how much he'd slipped into despair. "We're almost there. Any concerns before we arrive?"

He shook his head. "No, no questions or concerns." An impish look came to his features, brightening his brown eyes by a shade. They were almost golden in the light filtering through the windshield. "That was a question, so technically I get to ask another."

"Fine." I gave in, his brightened expression making the sting hurt less.

"If I get this—when I get this new arm—are you gonna run with me?"

It was my turn to look over in surprise, and I nearly missed our exit, jerking over at the last second. "Yeah, sure, why not? Beats running around with Taylor. That man cheats, let me tell you. Stupid cat claws."

He laughed. For the first time in my presence, he laughed, and something about the sound curled warm in my stomach, making me want to hear more of it.

"I believe it. He tries to sneak up on me sometimes at the shop. At first, I figured he was trying to catch me stealing or something, but he doesn't know he's doing it."

"He's always been light on his feet. I served with the team for a brief stint. A couple missions here and there when I was active duty. He was always the quiet one of the bunch. Besides, believe me, if he thought you were stealing, you'd be out on your ass."

"Yeah..." His smile remained. "I guess he would."

I risked another glance over while we were at a red light. "You should laugh more often, by the way. A sense of humor always helps."

His cheeks colored, and after clearing his throat, he fixed his attention on the window. "So, uh, I guess you being one of them means you could hand me my ass even if I had two hands?"

I snorted. "Doubtful. I'm a trained medic, not a combat soldier. My involvement with Ian's team was purely in a support role."

Shifting in the seat to look out the window, Lyle watched the city scenery with large, interested eyes. Now he reminded me of a hound, an intrigued dog waiting to hang his head out the window. The visual in my head made me giggle as I took us to the VA hospital, and he glanced at me, raising a brow.

"What's so funny?"

"Nothing," I said quickly.

After a skeptical look, he resumed looking. And lowered the window. I grinned wide at the change in my surly patient. Finally. Progress.

I pulled into a parking spot. "All right, look, before we head in there, I want to give you a heads up. A few of the doctors might not be so happy. I'm an outsider with connections, coming into their hospital and doing what I want. Ignore it. Don't say anything. I have enough pull that I have the MRI machine booked with only specific personnel allowed inside. People cleared by Ian, you understand? I'm going to get an image of your brain in both forms, then I'm going to delete the data from the system."

"Okay," he said, snickering. "So top secret military doctors are going to watch you scan a dog in an MRI. This'll be interesting."

7

JULIA

*A*s predicted by Lyle, the MRI became a hilarious experience. Hours later, while perusing his results at the clinic, I yawned and checked my mobile phone to see a text message from Russ inviting me to dinner.

Now.

As in, put down whatever the hell I was doing and come on down to eat while everything was hot. I rolled my eyes and was in the middle of Swyping an answer back to him when my office door unceremoniously swung open and six feet of blonde stepped inside. The scent of lioness invaded my office.

"What are you doing here?" I cried as I bounced from behind the desk and into Sasha's arms for a hug.

"I came to kidnap you," she announced. "Russ didn't believe you would take a break from work on your own, so I've been sent to drag you away."

Doctor Sasha Vogt, combat medic for Ian's team,

was the best friend I'd ever had next to my twin. We hadn't seen each other since Charles's funeral, and a scalding rush of shame flooded my face for running away from my friends when they'd tried to support me afterward.

I'd been such a mess. Talked to them so little since then.

But still, nothing improved the quality of a day like a visit from the best friend. Since my arrival in Texas, I had every intention of visiting her, but adapting this prosthetic to fit Lyle had taken over my life.

"Oh, such a friendly welcome from someone who was in Houston today without paying a visit to *me.*"

Leaning back to gaze up at her, I made a face and scrunched my nose. "Seriously? I couldn't stop by with my patient in the car."

"And why not? I've met Lyle before. I saved his life that day, after all. Maybe I'd like to see him again, too, and know how he has recovered. How is he?"

"Goodness, where do I begin? I mean, physically he appears to be in exceptional condition."

"But mentally?"

"He's depressed. I see it sometimes. Today seemed especially rough for him, but he came around by the time we reached Houston."

"I gotta say, I'm a bit surprised at your choice of patient, but I trust your judgement." She waited a beat, then added, "And Ian's. Mostly."

"Thanks. Off from working at the hospital today?"

Sasha flashed me a bright smile. "What do you

think? I told them I have a good friend to visit and not
to count on me accepting calls either for the next two
or three days. Unless your timeline is critical—which I
am most certain it is not—you and I will be spending
some time together seeing the sights Texas has to
offer."

"Sasha—"

"No arguments. You need a night or two away from
Quickdraw. Besides, I brought you clothes."

My eyebrows popped up toward my hairline, and
she laughed at me.

"On top of her writing, Nandi has decided to sell
clothes, so I've brought a care package from her."

For the first time since she entered, I scoped out her
casual wardrobe. She wore tight black leggings with
little stylistic rosebuds printed on them and a gray, off
the shoulder blouse, braless beneath it because she'd
hated them for as long as I could remember and was
small enough to pull it off.

Her hair swayed over one shoulder in a tidy fishtail
braid, colored the near-white shade of blonde women
paid at a salon to have. Nothing had changed about her
over the years, as flawless as she'd been the day we met
ten years ago.

"Okay, okay. Let me grab my things."

After shutting the laptop and packing my equipment, I joined Sasha in her car and squealed when she
produced a swollen, oversized tote bag stuffed with
fashionable delights.

My care package consisted of leggings with a

feather print on them, much bolder in color and pattern than Sasha's, with a long, black knit sweater and a pair of fuzzy calf-high boots. Digging deeper I found two more pairs of leggings, some jewelry, and several deluxe sized makeup samplers.

"What's all this?"

"We have so many subscription things that we figured you could try some of the doubles. Just because you're a doctor with fabulous skin genetics doesn't mean you can't put on makeup now and again."

Sasha lived in a penthouse apartment with two other successful lioness shifters. And they happened to be in a polyamorous relationship together, a pride without a male. Not for their lack of trying.

A few years ago, Taylor had been their male, and it had worked until Sasha and Nandi got the baby bug. With their biological clocks ticking and him being a cougar—not the male lion they needed—they'd all realized they were only putting off the inevitable.

I'd been her shoulder to cry on when they finally let go. The breakup, while amicable, had hurt everyone involved, and yet it had been a necessary evil.

Interbreeding between certain types of big cats never provided healthy offspring, and when it came to shifters, the results were the same. As a coyote, I had options ranging from my fellow coyote shifters to werewolves and dog shifters like Lyle. Charles and I even knew a coydog shifter while growing up on the reservation.

During our last discussion, Sasha had confided

their consideration of an anonymous donor dad now
that she was approaching her forty-second birthday. It
was hard enough finding a soulmate for a single
person, let alone someone to bond with three.

About ten minutes later, we cruised by Ian's house
where Leigh and Sophia were playing in the yard. They
waved to us in passing, and then we reached the end of
the lane where Russ lived in a modest, three-bedroom
cabin he'd built with his own hands from the ground to
the roof. Barking with enthusiasm, Trigger raced down
the steps to greet us when we approached the wood
fence and entered the gate.

"Hey there, good boy. I swear you're more handsome every time I see you." Excitement overtook Russ's
German shepherd with such intensity his entire body
wiggled along with his tail. I had to rub his neck a few
times before he left me alone, and even then he
bounded up and down the stairs as if to ask if we were
coming or not.

"Where's Russ?"

"Probably inside with the kids and waiting for us,"
Sasha replied.

In shifters, few things were more intense than the
need to breed. Sooner or later, we all got this feeling
telling us it was time to spread our genes around and
procreate, making more of our kind in a world where
we were in the 0.25% minority. And Russ had found a
wife who shared his outlook toward family.

When we stepped into their home, a sense of bliss
washed over me, as if the cabin was infused with the

warmth of its owners' love for their children. I grinned when I saw the toddler shoes between a pair of enormous boots and smaller, rhinestone-decorated flip flops. After removing our shoes, we passed a bucket of Legos and a bin of toys on our way to the kitchen.

"Hi, guys. We're he—" I started to call out.

Russ turned the corner and ran into us. Literally. I bounced off his huge chest then scowled at him. He towered over me by about six inches, his broad shoulders stretching a buttoned shirt tucked into the kind of jeans I'd admired on Lyle.

With the same stupid belt buckle. Texas men.

"Why don't you watch where you're going?" I demanded.

"It's my house. Anyway, about time you got here. I'm starving." Russ rubbed his flat, hard belly with exaggeration. Retirement hadn't done any damage to his waistline. Or the rest of him for that matter.

Sasha stood behind me and laughed while I sputtered up at him, hands on my hips.

"What?" he asked.

"I was coming, you big hairy jerk." I smacked him in the arm, not budging him at all.

"Oh yeah, sure you were. By around nine o'clock tonight after leftovers are in the fridge and I'm in bed asleep."

I wrinkled my nose at him. "You and Ian with your old man bedtimes. I swear."

"Hey, you sleep when the kids sleep. Otherwise you never get any," his wife said as she stepped up alongside him, cradling their nine-month-old daughter in her arms. "I made more of that apple pie you enjoyed."

"Figured we'd surprise you with a good dinner. I know Leigh's a damn good cook, but she's all into that healthy living crap lately. Poor Ian is over there living on salads and avocado." Russ grimaced for his friend's plight.

"Well, I'm here. I'm surprised by your kidnapping cohort"—I jerked my thumb over my shoulder toward the lioness—"and it smells delicious. Is that salmon?"

"Yup. Been smoking it all day once I found out you two were comin' down to dinner. I figured fish is something even a picky eater like Sasha can't turn down." Russ grinned at us before disappearing into the kitchen.

"Here, Dani, I'll take Olivia for you," Sasha offered. "Where's Mateo?"

"Asleep in his room. Poor guy has a cold, so he munched on some oatmeal and climbed into bed. Out like a light."

"Aww, poor little dude," I said. "Want one of us to check on him?"

Dani opened her mouth to reply, but Russ bellowed from the kitchen, beating her to it. "Yes, please!"

After the three of us women shared a laugh, I went to check in on Mateo so Sasha could get in her baby fix with Olivia.

"She's gotten so big," was the last thing I heard Sasha croon before I stepped out of hearing range and into Mateo's quiet room.

Surrounded by stuffed animals and Pokemon plushes, their little boy slept in his racecar-themed child bed with a nearby nightlight casting animal shapes on the wall.

One perk about being a shifter was we never stayed sick for long. A quick listen to his breathing and a peek inside his mouth assured me he'd be fine. Nothing a little honey, rest, and cuddling couldn't fix. He barely stirred through my mini-examination.

After running my fingers through his bed-tousled dark hair, I exited the room and joined the adults in the kitchen.

"He'll survive," I announced. "Make him some honey pops. He'll love that. Just don't let Russ get to them first."

I avoided a snap from the towel in Russ's hands and danced away to the dinner table.

Dani made an amazing dinner that pushed the limit of my dietary plan, but I wolfed down seconds and attempted thirds anyway. Russ must have told her cheesy risotto was my Kryptonite, because she wrapped up refrigerator containers with a generous heap of leftovers to take back to Houston for everyone. Between the smoked salmon, parmesan risotto, asparagus, fresh garlic bread, and dessert, I thought Russ and Sasha would have to roll me out to her car.

"More wine?" Dani offered.

I waved my hands at her and shook my head. Although the honey and floral taste was delicious, especially when paired with her blackberry apple crumble, I couldn't safely get down another sip.

"I'm probably gonna pass out on Sasha during the drive back."

We made a pit stop at Ian and Leigh's place to get my carry-on and drop off my work equipment. Dani had sent us over with an extra pie for them as well.

The last thing I remembered was reaching the end of his road, and then suddenly our journey was over and we were surrounded by the cement and brick walls of an underground parking garage. A bleary glance at the clock told me over an hour had passed.

Either Sasha drove like a bat out of hell or the traffic had been substantially less than when I drove Lyle. Probably a mix of both. I wiped the drool off my mouth and stretched in the seat, creaking back and neck protesting the sudden movement.

"You snort in your sleep. I forgot how cute that was," she teased.

"I don't," I mumbled.

We rode a private elevator to the top, and the moment we entered, Isisa, one of Sasha's girls, turned the corner into the foyer to greet us.

Her amber eyes lit up with joy before she rushed over to fold me into her arms. "Julia! Hi, girl. It's about time you came to see us."

"I was abducted against my will," I quipped.

"Russ and Ian said she works herself to death, so I've dragged her away from her project for a few days."

Nandi peered down from the upper level and

squealed. A few seconds later, she came rushing down the stairs and beelined over to join the hug, trapping me between the two stronger, taller lionesses.

They were gorgeous, and if I went that way, I'd probably wiggle into their pride, but more importantly than their looks, they'd clawed and scratched their way into successful careers. Isisa had a partnership at a flourishing law firm that specialized in helping abused spouses and children. Nandi wrote and independently published romance novels, the most recent of which had hit the *USA Today* Best-Sellers list. They'd all come over from South Africa together years ago.

"This place is gorgeous," I murmured as I stepped farther inside.

"It suits us." Isisa smiled and skipped over to their large, open kitchen. Contrasting Nandi's plump curves, Isisa had a sleek, athletic build, the kind of body I'd expect on a tennis player instead of a lawyer. She moved like a weightless sprite, all grace and long, lithe limbs. "Wine? Beer? Something stronger?"

"Oh no, no. Just water for me. Russ and Dani pushed me to my limit already. Where should I toss my stuff in the meantime?"

"Um. We have a fourth room, but…" Nandi's voice trailed.

"It's kind of the junk room where Sasha keeps all this crap we cannot put anywhere else. There isn't a bed," Isisa explained.

A room for the mate they yearned to have one day. I didn't pray often, but I'd make an exception if it meant nudging fate their direction, because if anyone deserved to find the man of their dreams, it was these three women.

I offered to sleep on the couch until Isisa insisted it wasn't necessary and guided me to her bedroom instead. Despite being soulbonded mates, the girls each kept a personal space. They were still lionesses after all, each with her own quirks and differences.

As I was lying in bed, I thought if I was aching for a mate, then certainly the girls, who were already a few years ahead of me and in their early forties, were close to desperate.

Losing Charles had shaken my faith, but for the first time in months, I prayed to any god or goddess out there listening, even the forces of nature itself. It didn't matter who, as long as my three friends found the future they deserved.

8

LYLE

*A*fter studying my MRI results, Julia had determined I'd be a perfect candidate for the program. I received my temporary prosthetic a few days later, and with a bit of practice over the next week, learned to pick up a beer can with it.

Everybody has to start somewhere, right?

There was nothing special about this arm, but Julia called it practice, mental training as well as physical, much like a person cutting down their food intake while preparing to undergo gastric bypass. I used it to polish the windows in Taylor's auto shop and wipe the counters, but mostly I tried to train myself into the habit of using both hands again. I'd grown dependent on my right and accustomed to the loss.

"Hey. We're all going out to Sally's tonight for the fried chicken. You coming?" T-Bone called from the door.

"Yeah, sure." The local diner had the best fried chicken in east Texas, and the burgers weren't bad either, so I called home and let Mama know to stay off her feet.

"Hey, don't cook anything. I'm buying dinner from Sally's."

"Oh, great. Bring home a gallon of sweet tea, too, baby."

"Will do. Love you, Ma."

I hung up as Taylor emerged from the office on his way to the storeroom, a clipboard in his hand. He paused to glance at me. "Personal calls during work hours?"

Shit. As soon as I began to panic, he grinned and continued along on his way. "Just messing with you. Keep making me money the way you do, and you can call whoever you want."

I grumbled under my breath about cats being assholes.

He disappeared into the next room just as another of the guys popped out from the garage. "Yo. You really coming to hang with us tonight?"

"Yeah."

"Good. Hank's boy will be out on the patio with his band, and Luis is bringing some girls 'round for dancing. It's gonna be a good night."

"Sounds like a plan."

"Oh, hey, can you call up Mr. Turner and let him know his car will be another half hour? We found a nail in the tire."

"Sure thing." I waved him off to the garage and plucked up the phone, knocking my mug with the artificial limb. Coffee sloshed over the rim.

"Crap," I muttered, reaching for a rag.

Mr. Turner answered, so I passed on the message about his car then hung up.

The chime above the door tinkled, and a husky, feminine voice crooned, "Well, look who's back in town."

I cringed. My spine stiffened and my stomach twisted, but I forced a neutral smile on my face before spinning to face the woman in the shop's doorway.

Drugs had spoiled Angie's looks the way age dulls a Renaissance painting or heat ruins a wax figure. She could have been a model after high school, but getting strung out on heroin had screwed her chances of making that dream come true. A few heavy layers of makeup tried to conceal the damage she'd done to herself over the years, a shitty facade for a spiteful, whiny girl. The foundation settled into wrinkles and creases as deep as canyons, and purple track marks littered her forearms.

Looking at her now, I wondered what I'd ever seen in her.

"Mornin', Angie."

"Really? 'Mornin', Angie' is all you got to say to me, baby?" She leaned forward in a way that pushed her breasts together between her arms. They practically popped out of her tank top, resembling two hard melons shoved beneath her skin.

Fake. Not sure how she afforded it. Told myself I didn't care. Before prison, before all that crap went down with Tito and Taylor, I'd have taken Angie to the bathroom and given her a quick fuck and shared a smoke afterward no matter what she looked like.

That wasn't my life anymore.

"Got no reason to say much else," I told her. "If you aren't here as a customer, I'm gonna ask you to clear on out."

Her green eyes widened. "Excuse me?"

"You heard me. This ain't a hang-out spot anymore, and you won't find any drugs here. This is a legit business with actual paying customers. So, unless you have a car that needs fixing, I suggest you get on outta here." Hell, I was the one who was gone for three years. She had to already know that.

Rubbing my clammy palm against my jeans, I nervously shot a glance over my shoulder toward the narrow hall leading to the stockroom. What if Taylor came out and found me talking to her?

"I came to see my boyfriend now that he's out of jail. Not that you bothered to come see me," she pouted.

"Angie, we were never together like that. We fucked and we shot up. That's it, and I ain't doing that garbage no more." Getting clean in prison was the best thing that could have ever happened to me.

"I waited three years for you, and that's all you got to say to me?"

"You know damn well you ain't waited three years for me," I bit out, finally raising my voice. "Now clear the hell out of here before I—"

The door chime rang again, and my blood ran cold when I saw our visitor. Julia stepped in and paused to take in the bizarre scene in front of her—a crazy store clerk shouting wildly at a customer. I was probably flushed too. I blushed easy, and when something pissed me off, everything above my shirt flared red. I lowered the arm I was sweeping toward the door in a gesture for Angie to leave.

"Hey, sorry. Am I interrupting?" Julia looked between me and Angie.

"Nah, doc, she was just leaving."

"Like hell I was," Angie snapped.

Julia's gaze washed over me from head to toe, no doubt taking in my tense posture and reddened face. If she'd been standing outside of the door during my argument, she caught the last words exchanged between us, too.

Through the glass window separating the repair center from the storefront, a few of the guys watched us.

"You need to go," Julia said. "The owner of this place doesn't appreciate solicitation, and I imagine he'll be happy to call the sheriff if you're unwilling to comply with his clerk's polite directive. He asked you several times to leave."

"Who the hell are you? His mother?" Angie looked

Julia over in a manner I knew all too well. She was sizing her up, determining if she was a threat.

"A friend," Julia replied. She offered a pleasant smile, maintaining her cool in the face of Angie's blatant antagonism.

"Whatever." Angie spun on her heel and crossed toward the door. She paused beside Julia. "Go ahead and keep him, then, honey. Not like he could fuck worth a damn anyway *before* he lost his arm. You go ahead and keep the mangled bastard."

The door slammed shut behind her and rattled in its frame. Mortified by her behavior, I took my anger out on the counter by spraying cleaner then scrubbing the lemon-fresh puddle left behind.

Julia crossed over and set her hand down over mine.

"Come on," she said. "Let's get out of here."

"Still got an hour," I mumbled without meeting her eye.

"Go ahead, man. Doc trumps boss," Taylor called from the doorway to the garage. He'd probably heard every damn word said. Stupid cats and their sharp ears. "We'll meet up later with you at Sally's."

With no other options available, I followed Julia outside. The heatwave had finally broke, bringing a heavenly, cool autumn breeze.

Julia didn't press for conversation. Side by side, we wandered down the street in silence while I trained my gaze on the concrete. I had no idea where we were headed, nor did I care. After a block or two, my anger dimmed, and we crossed the street by the post office to make our way toward the park.

"The sergeant who was supposed to get the limb replacement," Julia said, breaking the silence, "was my brother."

I snapped my gaze toward her. It was the last thing I expected, the news bringing a swell of sympathy and understanding. "I didn't know. I'm sorry."

She nodded, pursed her lips, then continued. "Charles and I were close, and after he lost his arm overseas, I made it my priority to find a way to give him back his mobility. I'd already made headway with this new synthetic metal as well as drawn blueprints for different prosthetics. Charles was the motivation I needed to truly make it work."

Fuck, she was a genius, and I was deluded if I thought my one-sided puppy love crush was ever going to amount to something.

"What happened? I mean, how did—" I flushed and shook my head, realizing how personal of a question it was. "Sorry, it's none of my business."

"Suicide," she confided in her soft voice. "He missed an appointment, and when I went to go check on him, well, I found him in the garage with the engine running, an empty bottle of vodka in his lap."

Shit.

"He'd given up, Lyle, and I didn't see all the signs. I spent months blaming myself for not noticing." She paused and wet her lips, large brown eyes focused on the autumnal landscape nearby. "But I don't anymore."

"You worried I'm gonna go the same way?"

Julia stopped and turned to face me. The cool wind tousled her hair around her face and carried her soft-spoken words to me on a gentle breeze. "Not anymore. You worried me the other week when you were quiet in the car. And I hope if you do start to feel that way, you'll come and talk to me. Talk to Ian. Even Taylor if you have to. Because whether you believe it or not, you'd be missed."

"Doc—"

She held up a hand. "Not only because you're my subject, but because you're a friend. Anyway, I wanted to tell you not to allow people like your old acquaintance back there to get you down. You're not mangled, Lyle, and even if you weren't getting this arm, you'd be getting by fine. Look at everything you've accomplished since leaving prison."

In that moment, looking at her, I really believed it. She didn't look at me with pity or false praise, only admiration and…something I hadn't expected to see from the beautiful doctor. Attraction.

As we stood facing each other on the sidewalk, I resisted the insane urge to take her in my arms and kiss her. Her gaze flicked down to my lips then back up to my eyes, and she leaned forward ever so slightly, everything about her body language inviting me in. My fingers skimmed the edge of her light jacket, curling into the fabric, ready to tug her closer.

"Hey, Lyle! Come play ball with us!"

And just like that, the moment was shattered, and

the world around us came back into focus. Three kids —either oblivious or cockblocking bastards—from my group stood a few feet away. One had a basketball in his hands.

"Come on. I'll be your cheerleader," Julia said, stepping away.

9

JULIA

According to Lyle, he'd played varsity on the high school basketball team, and he'd kept up his skills while in prison. Eager to see him in action that didn't involve weights or physical rehabilitation exercises, I moved over to the sidelines.

"Come play with us!" Lyle called.

I shook my head and held out both hands. "Nooo, no. I don't do basketball."

The kids playfully booed me, but I stood my ground while they argued over who teamed up with their mentor. This was an entirely new side of Lyle that I'd seen only in glimpses before. He was good with the boys, laughing and joking around like a genuine role model and not the ex-con I'd expected to meet.

It came down to a couple games of rock-paper-scissors, and the kid named Kevin won the privilege of teaming with Lyle. He looked positively euphoric, like it was his birthday, Christmas, and every other holiday rolled into one massive gift.

They traveled up and down the court, Lyle making the best of his so-called handicap with one functional hand and a prosthetic. He had a strong bounce pass, and his innate shifter reflexes rarely let the ball past him. After a while, I stopped watching him with a clinical eye and started admiring his grace instead. His muscles rippled beneath his T-shirt, the cotton stretched taut over his muscles when Kevin encouraged him to go for a dunk.

"Man, how do you move so fast and do all that with one arm?" one of the other boys demanded.

"Practice," Lyle replied, grinning. "If I can do all this with one arm, there's no excuse for you, li'l man. You better have a place on that team next year."

"Are you going to keep working with me?" Kevin asked.

"Sure, Kev. I'll meet up with you here when I get out of TJ's shop Saturday."

His eyes lit up. "Really?"

"Yeah. That's no problem."

"Sweet!"

The other two teens, Brett and Jason, pleaded with Lyle for permission to tag along, too, and by the end, he'd been roped into gaming with all three of them each weekend. After he agreed, two of the boys grabbed skateboards, and another fetched his bike.

"See you Saturday, man."

We split and went our own direction, meandering back toward Taylor's shop where I left my car.

"You're really good with them," I said.

He grinned. "Yeah. I guess Ian knew what he was doing when he offered me the opportunity to help out with them. Most of the kids come from good families and all, but…"

"But?" I gently prompted.

"Kevin's father doesn't treat him so well, he says. Kinda blows him off and doesn't do shit with him." He shrugged.

"He told you that?"

Lyle nodded, and a flush came over his face. "I asked him one day why he got busted shoplifting from the grocery store in town. He said he just wanted his pops to pay attention to him, you know?"

"It's nice they feel like they can talk to you. You can really help make a difference in their lives."

"S'pose so." The same flush remained, as red as his hair.

I grinned and nudged him in the ribs with my elbow. "It's cute when you blush. You know, you're awfully soft for a hardened criminal."

He snorted. "Anyway, that's why I do it. I wish I had somebody like Ian around when I was a kid. Maybe I wouldn't have started doping up in high school." He gazed at the dimmed storefront of the automotive shop with a deep crease in his forehead, drawing his brows close together. "Maybe I would have gone to college."

"It's not too late to go to college."

"I'm almost thirty. I think college days are over."

"You'd be surprised how many older students are enrolled. You could even take online courses to suit your work schedule."

"I haven't been to school in years." He dragged his hand through his hair and frowned. "I guess it's an option though. One day."

"Lucky for you, getting an education is a door that never really closes. So keep it in mind."

"Yeah, I will. Thanks. Maybe when you're all done playing Doctor Frankenstein with me, yeah?"

"Then apply for the spring semester at… What's close to Quickdraw?"

"Sam Houston."

"Good school?"

He shrugged and leaned against my car. "It's got a few good programs, but I'd probably go for business or accounting once you give me the okay."

"You'll be using two arms again by Christmas and able to crunch all the numbers you want," I told him. "When you're not playing ball with the boys. But I want you to know something first, all right?"

"What's that?"

"It's okay to change your mind," I said quietly, gazing up at him. "This arm is a tool, and only a tool. It doesn't make you any better a man, and lacking it doesn't make you any less of one. And I'm not going to be disappointed in you if the risks freak you out."

He nodded and scuffed the edge of a shoe against the ground. "I know, Julia. Took me a while to realize it, but I know."

Julia. He'd finally said my name.

I smiled at him and touched his shoulder. "Then don't forget it."

My thoughts drifted back to that moment on the sidewalk near the recreation center, positive he meant to kiss me if the kids hadn't interrupted us. What troubled me wasn't his growing infatuation—it was the mutual attraction flourishing each time we were together.

"Any idea when the surgery will be?" he asked, jarring me from my thoughts.

"In a couple weeks. That's actually why I came by the garage. I wanted to let you know I'd scheduled a date with the hospital."

"Wow." He ran his hand through his hair and chuckled. "I guess I didn't think it'd be so soon, you know?"

"I figured you'd want to be coherent and pain free for Thanksgiving. This way you'll have some time to recover before stuffing yourself with food, then we can work on adjustments up until Christmas. It won't be perfect at first."

"Seems like a pretty good gift," he said. "Having my arm back."

I dropped him off at Sally's and declined his invitation to join them inside. He deserved a night out with his friends without his doctor hanging around.

Even if it killed me to let him go, because deep

down, the stirring attraction between us told me stealing Lyle away for the night was the thing we both needed but could never have.

He was my patient, and being in lust with him couldn't take precedence over a medical breakthrough.

10

LYLE

With Julia on my mind all night, I couldn't sleep worth a damn. I was afraid the restless tossing and turning on the living room sofa would wake Mama, so I ran in dog form for a while outside, dressed again, and eventually meandered into town.

I had the keys to Taylor's shop. He and Jada had business out of town, and T-Bone needed to be in Huntsville to tour the university campus.

It felt like a test, one last trial to see if I'd fuck anything up, fall back on my old ways, rob him blind and risk the ass-beating not only from him, but from Russ and T-Bone if I betrayed his trust.

Yeah, I wasn't that dumb.

Working for Taylor was a thousand times better than being Tito's loyal hound, and while I missed my friend at times, I didn't miss the way he'd treated me.

Because like I'd told the kids at the club, we

deserved more than a handful of shitty friends, and the sooner we acknowledged it, the better.

As the hour approached midnight, I took inventory in the supply room, but kept the lights dim to avoid drawing unwanted attention to the shop. I'd already punched in the alarm passcode, but with my luck, some friendly member of the QPD would decide I was robbing the place and haul me off in cuffs.

A soft, muted thump sounded from the side door of the junkyard. Metal dinged against metal, and Luis's toolkit—I knew it was his because Taylor and T-Bone were always telling him to lock it up—clattered to the ground in the garage.

Someone was in the shop. Of all the nights to try this bullshit, someone chose the evening I was crouched in the rear of the stockroom, holding a clipboard beside a pile of alternators and spark plug boxes.

Had I left one of the doors unlocked, or was that Luis's fuck-up since he'd been the last out of the garage. Either way, someone was in a place where they didn't belong, and I had two options.

My gaze darted to the telephone on the wall then to a few auto parts I could improvise into a weapon. Nah. I didn't want to hurt anyone. But I would protect Taylor's property.

Deciding to play the part of the junkyard dog to scare them off, I removed all my clothes and shifted, glad I'd left the prosthetic at home. Contorting myself into my hound shape, I lowered to three paws and padded to the door. I'd left it partially ajar, no doubt revealing a sliver of light beyond the stockroom.

"Where the hell would the good shit be? What if it's locked up?" someone whispered in the dark.

"Maybe in the back somewhere… My dad had to buy some parts the other day, and that idiot Lyle moved around the corner and through this door."

"Hey, guys, there's a light on back there. I don't think we're alone."

I charged out. Even on three legs, barking and snarling like a rabid animal, I knew how to strike fear into a group of junior thugs. The boys split and dashed away, and I was content to let them—until I recognized the slim, lanky shape of Kevin and smelled him beneath the oversized black hoodie.

Something wild and crazed came over me, because Ian said this kid had only one more chance and then it was kiddie incarceration. In a fury, I bit the heavy denim around his ankle and yanked, taking him off balance and down to the ground. He screamed and kicked, flailing at me while crying out for help. The four guys with him hauled ass. One lingered, as if on the fence about rescuing his pal, but he dashed out the door and they were gone.

Some friends.

"Don't kill me, don't kill me!" He dissolved into a sobbing mess, almost hysterical.

I hadn't bit him once. Realizing that, his cries subsided after a few moments, and his confused gray eyes raised to my face. To appear docile and unintimidating now, I touched the kid with my whiskers and tickled him.

It did the trick, because he laughed between the rest of his hiccups and dying sobs.

"Hey. You're missing a leg. You're not so vicious, are you?"

Perceptive even when whimpering and crying himself into a snotty mess.

He rubbed behind my ears with the experienced fingers of a kid accustomed to handling a big dog. "I wonder if Taylor picked you up because of Lyle."

I *am* Lyle. I envied the ravens and some of our other brethren who were able to talk regardless of shape.

Struck with indecision, I waited long enough to weigh my options before going with the reckless choice. I paced away from him a few steps and shifted. From eighty-five pounds of dog to one hundred and ninety pounds of standing man.

"Now I figure we both got an awful lot to explain to each other," I said, leaning down to offer him a hand up from the floor.

"What the...but you—"

"Turn into a dog and back again. Yeah, I know. Go sit over there while I grab my jeans. You try to ditch and I will run you the fuck down and drag you to the police department by your throat." I pointed to the couch in the waiting area, tensed and waiting to see if he called my bluff.

Kevin hurried to the seats and was still sitting there when I came back. Good.

"You wanna tell me what you were doing here tonight?"

"You wanna tell me how the hell you turned into a dog?!"

"Okay, fair." A few moments of silence passed between us after I sat beside him. He didn't flinch at least, as if I was a leper or some monster. "You first, kid. Then you can ask me your questions. Now, what were you doing here, and who all was with you?"

"Man, I ain't no snitch."

"You can tell me or Sheriff MacArthur."

"I'll tell him what you—"

"What makes you think he doesn't already know? Look, I saw what happened, dude. Your buddies bounced and left you here to get mauled. Are those real friends? Those the kind of people you want to protect with *your* freedom? There's loyal, and then there's dumb. I've been both before."

His shoulders drooped. "I didn't wanna do it."

"Who were the others?"

"Manuelo, Eddie, Jed, and Caleb."

"Jed, that's the one who was messing with you and Brett."

Kevin nodded and stared down at his feet. Time passed, but it wasn't an awkward lull, before he whispered, "You must hate me now. I let you down."

"Nah, man. I don't hate you. I'm disappointed you let them push you into this shit, but I don't hate you. Look, everybody makes mistakes, but you can't keep making the same one like this."

"Are you going to tell on me?"

"Nah." I shook my head. "I'd like for you to go to Sheriff MacArthur or even visit Chief Blackstone yourself, but I'm not gonna turn you in."

"They'll throw me into TYC, man."

"Not if you go and talk to the sheriff yourself. Tell him the whole truth about this kid Jed."

"Can I have some time to think on it?"

As far as I could see, the kids hadn't caused any damage to the property or taken anything trespassing.

"Yeah, sure. All they did was take a walk in here really. My bad for leaving most of the locks unsecured."

I'd leave the surveillance footage though. Taylor would want to see it, and the likelihood of convincing him to do things my way made me confident he'd hold off on reporting the boys to the police.

"Did you bust up Mr. George's shop?"

"No, but Jed did it. Bragged about the money he made selling stuff. He, uh, he said we'd make a ton grabbing stuff from the garage."

"That why you did this? For money?"

"Not at first. I told him no, but…"

"He kept pushing." I remembered how that worked. My so-called friends had reigned me into all sorts of trouble when I was younger. Then, one day, I became the bully doing the pressuring. "C'mon. I'll walk you home."

After arming the alarm system, I escorted the teen outside into the cool, nighttime breeze. Street lamps lit our way down the highway road running parallel to the railroad tracks bisecting Quickdraw. Choices took drivers north toward Tyler or south to Houston. We'd have to cross the tracks to reach our respective neighborhoods.

"I don't do drugs, so I know I didn't hallucinate in there," Kevin began after a few minutes of silence. "What are you? An alien or something?"

The question made me laugh. "Nah, not an alien. Trust me."

"So are you like a werewolf, then? Except a dog?"

"Pretty much. I'm a shapeshifter. I inherited it from my dad, and there's a lot of other people like me out there who turn into other animals. Some of them live in this town."

More than a few, but I wasn't going to elaborate. I was pretty sure Ian would give me some sort of stern lecture if he found out about this.

"Really?" His eyes widened and gleamed with unveiled admiration.

I grinned back at him before nodding. "Yep, but I can't tell you who. It's kinda against our unspoken rules." I'd outted Taylor to Tito because back then it was my job to inform him of any shifters who moved into town.

"Guess this means I can't tell anyone."

"I'd appreciate it, yeah. If it means anything to you, I'm impressed you didn't piss your pants and freak out." Aside from his initial outburst, Kevin had taken it in stride.

"Yeah, well, I was kind of thankful to be alive and not starring in my own version of *Cujo*."

Idle chitchat about my life as a shifter entertained him along the fifteen-minute walk into the subdivision where he lived with his mother, father, and little sister. The family dwelled in a single-wide trailer in need of a fresh coat of white paint, the original job peeling off the wood-rotted shutters.

Mark Wilson used to drive trucks for a living, in and out of their lives for days at a time. Recently, he had sold his rig and traded his old occupation for the life of a farmer. Mark's pickup was out front beside a battered old coupe.

"Anyone know you're gone?"

The porch light was off and the windows dim, the trailer too quiet.

"I snuck out after Mom and Dad went to bed. He's still asleep, I think…" He breathed an audible sigh of relief, and I thought back to the bruises he sometimes had on his arms and face.

Injuries on the basketball court, he'd claimed when I inquired. Now I wasn't so sure.

The only thing worse than a dad who wasn't there, was one who beat on his kids and hurt them.

"Remember what I said, Kevin. You have a choice here, and I can't help you if you decide to roll with Jed and his boys again."

"He's bigger than me."

The way he was eyeing his house, I had to wonder if he meant Jed, his father, or both.

"Meet me tomorrow at the garage when it closes. I'll show you some defensive moves I learned in prison."

"Really?"

"Yeah. But I want you to think about talking to the sheriff first. Either way, though, come on by, and I'll show you. Now, how you plan on getting inside?"

"My window."

It didn't take much to get him safely—and quietly—inside. Now all I had to do was hope he followed my advice and kept my secret.

After seeing Kevin safely home the previous night, I'd rounded back to Taylor's shop and checked the damage to the door. It wasn't awful. I easily replaced the busted lock and decided what, if anything, I'd tell Taylor.

The truth. I'd have to tell him the truth and warn the guys about checking every door when we closed up shop. As for the police, fear of getting Kevin pinched for trespassing, as well as attempted burglary, made me reluctant to phone it in.

In the meantime, someone had to watch over the shop, so I made it a habit of seeing Mama off to bed, napping, then checking in to Taylor's place by eleven.

On the fourth night, just in case they decided to round back again, I left the garage doors open while I organized the toolkits and cleaned the equipment, daring Jed or one of his homies to try robbing us again.

No one was man enough to try the shop with me here, so I worked in silence each night.

At the end of the week, moments after I decided to call it a night and close, a female coyote scurried into the garage. Although there was too much distance between us for me to get a good whiff of her scent, I couldn't imagine any other coyote wandering boldly around civilization. I grinned and crossed over to her.

"Julia?"

She cocked her head.

Against every speck of common sense I had, I crouched down to her level and touched her face with my right hand, skimming my fingertips over her furry cheek. She leaned into it and closed her eyes.

"Damn, you're awfully pretty."

Brown fur in shades of caramel and gold covered her slim body with the occasional cream or black streak. She was lithe, taller than I'd expected, with a narrow muzzle and large brown eyes. And she was growing her winter coat. The fur was plush beneath my hand, almost inviting me to rest my face against her throat.

Straightening, I resisted and gestured to the door behind me. "There's a clean pair of coveralls in my locker. Last one on the left. Help yourself."

Julia trotted through the only other open door and turned a sharp right into the staff room.

While she changed, I secured the doors and tried not to let my imagination run wild with fantasies of her naked in the next room with her long legs and sleek, smooth limbs.

Tiny as all get-out in my work clothes, Julia returned to the garage and flashed a big grin. "Thanks," she said, distracting me from my lecherous thoughts. She'd rolled the sleeves up over her elbows, but the legs puddled over her feet, revealing her bare toes. "I've been stretching my legs the past few nights. Since I live in the city, I never have the chance to run wild and free back home. Anyway, what are you doing here? It's the middle of the night."

"I couldn't sleep, so I did some work."

Her brows raised. "Every night?"

"How'd you know it was every night?"

Julia didn't break eye contact, and while I was tempted to glance away first, I didn't. I tried to tell myself the smoldering glow in her eyes was a trick of the light.

"Like I said, I've been stretching my legs, but I didn't want to bother you at work." She moistened her lips with the tip of her tongue, and I was entranced, struggling to look away.

"Bother me? You'd have to go out of your way to bother me, especially this late when there ain't a single customer. I just putter around here alone every night."

Her lips parted then shut again. "I...um. I saw you out with Kevin the other night. That's not exactly alone."

"You saw us?"

She shrugged then took a seat on the sofa and

clasped the edges of the cushions with both of her hands. "In passing."

Unable to lie to Julia's beautiful face, I decided to tell her the truth. Not just because I trusted her, but because it felt like fate had sent her for a reason like a guardian angel with brown fur able to give the advice I needed.

"Some kids broke into the garage a few nights ago," I told her. "Kevin was with them."

"I'm sorry. That must have been rough to discover."

"Yeah." I released a pent-up breath and rubbed my hand against the thigh of my jeans. "I ran out in my dog form and scared the shit out of them. Pinned Kevin before he could get away, and the other jackasses just left him. Just left him to get mauled or killed. Some friends, right?"

"Sounds like he was a fall guy for them."

"Yeah... They didn't get away with anything, and I fixed the door they damaged when they came in. Anyway, Kevin knows what I am, and he's scared shitless."

"I, uh, what?"

"Heh." Her wide, disbelieving eyes reminded me of a cartoon character. I expected them to bug out of her head at any second. "Yeah, I sorta decided a good shock might do him some good. Don't worry, I didn't tell him about the others, and it's not like anybody would *believe* him even if he did."

"No, that didn't even cross my mind. How did he take it though?"

"Surprisingly well, I guess. I know I should tell MacArthur about what happened, but I don't want Kevin to get in trouble," I said while kicking a loose screw on the ground. Focusing on my feet made it easier to tolerate her company, because every time she was near, I wanted to discover the taste of her skin and feel her soft body against mine.

"Well, if it were me, I'd give him the chance to do the right thing."

Swallowing a few times, I glanced out the window and asked in a quiet voice, "How long is long enough? A week? Two?"

She pursed her lips and wriggled her bare toes against the tiled floor. "How long has it been already? A week?"

I nodded.

"Is that why you've really been here each night? Waiting to see if they try again? Protect the place?"

"Yup, pretty much."

"And that's why you're tired during our appointments."

I grimaced. "Sorry."

"No, I admire your loyalty. Both to Kevin and to Taylor, but you can't take all of this upon yourself."

"Taylor comes back tomorrow from his vacation with Jada. I figured I'd tell him about the trespassing and let him take it from there." Omitting Kevin's name and hoping I could coax him into visiting Ian to tell the truth. Once he turned in Jed, Quickdraw could return to the quiet community we all knew before Tito moved into town years ago.

Silence fell between us while I studied the space between my booted feet. When I couldn't take another moment of it, just when I planned to apologize for taking up her time, Julia's warm palm touched my cheek and coaxed me to look at her.

"And if Kevin doesn't fess up on his own? What then? I know you want to protect him, but he also has to make his own choices."

"I dunno, Julia. I really don't. I know you're right, and when I look back, I sorta wish someone had taken a stand for me, even if it did mean ratting me out. Maybe I wouldn't have turned out so fucked up."

Her hand hadn't moved, skin soft against my unshaven jaw. Every time she touched me during our physical therapy sessions, I thought I'd combust from excitement.

"Your surgery is in four days, you know. Better if you weren't worried sick up to the date of the procedure."

"Yeah, I know. You're right."

"Talk to Taylor tomorrow. Talk to Kevin. Get it off your chest and put the ball in his court. Maybe…" Her thumb stroked across my cheek, slim fingers gliding down my neck. "Maybe you'll come home from the hospital to a pleasant surprise."

I struggled to look away from her eyes. It must have been mutual. Eventually, I tore my attention down to watch her bare feet shift, her breath quicken, and her thighs fall slightly apart.

God, she was bare under the coveralls. No panties or bra, just a thin layer of polyester blend, dark blue fabric covering what I imagined to be the most perfect female body in existence.

Fuck.

"Anyway, I better go. Thanks for loaning these to me."

She moved away first, dropping her hand and standing. As much as I hated to lose the contact between us, I did nothing to get it back, staying where I was. She disappeared to change, and before she ran out in her coyote form, she paused to nuzzle my knee before taking off into the night. I shut the door behind her and twisted the lock again.

With only a few hours until dawn, I stretched out on the couch and slept until the stench of feline invaded my senses and dragged me from sleep.

"Didn't expect to see you here this early." Taylor tilted his head and studied me.

"Oh, hey, man." I sat up.

"Looks like you need this more than me." Chuckling, Taylor offered a to-go cup of coffee from the bakery up the street.

After groggily rubbing my eyes, I took the cup in my right hand. "Thanks," I mumbled. "How was vacation?"

"It was good. Great. Almost didn't wanna come

back. Lemme tell ya, if you ever have a chance to enjoy a cruise, go for it.

"Nah, wouldn't be any fun alone." The coffee was like a scalding blessing. It burned me, but I sipped it anyway and hoped it'd be enough to power me through a long day at the counter and whatever therapeutic exercises Julia planned for me. The left side of my body ached with tension lately. I hadn't realized how dependent I'd become on my right until she had become my slave driver.

"So, how'd things go here? Taking shop management to new levels, huh?"

"Yeah, about that."

I caught him up on what happened but left out the names of the guilty parties. I'd already done a little work to discover the identities of all the teens involved, but the only one I wanted to burn was that asshole Jed for suckering them into it.

"And you let them go?" Taylor asked incredulously.

"Look, I'm gonna go see the one kid today. Try to give him one last chance to fess up himself. After that, I'll go straight to Ian. All right? I'm sorry, man. I just couldn't rat them out like that without talking to you first."

My confidence collapsed, and my thoughts turned grim with dark expectations.

He'd fire me. Maybe I could stock groceries after hours at the supermarket in town... I mean, I'd have two arms soon to do that at least, right? I could do that.

"Why do you think he did it? Better yet, why does it matter to you whether he gets picked up or not?"

"I think he was bullied into it, and I remember how that feels. That's why it matters. He's got a shitty home with a dad I think is beating on him and… I just couldn't."

Taylor's expression softened, and the hints of anger smoldering in his eyes dimmed. The taut stretch of his mouth relaxed, and his shoulders dropped. "All right. I'll trust your judgment, Lyle."

I blinked at him. "Just like that?"

"Yeah. Just like that." He maneuvered around to the water dispenser and filled a cup. "Besides, I have a hidden surveillance feed broadcasting to my phone through the Wi-Fi. I saw the entire thing the night it happened, but you handled it like a pro." Chuckling at my expression, Taylor disappeared into his office.

And then I knew without a doubt that placing the shop in my care during his vacation had been a test after all.

A test I had proudly passed.

11

LYLE

*F*all. My favorite time of the year, and it had nothing to do with pumpkin spice lattes. Okay. A little. The guys at TJ's shop liked to joke about me being a basic bitch trapped in a man's body, but they couldn't shame me from enjoying the world's rush to produce pumpkin *everything*.

I stepped into Quickdraw's only cafe and let the smell of seasonal baked goods surround me.

"Good evening, Lyle," Mrs. Tyler called out to me from behind the counter. "Haven't seen you in a while. What can I get for you, dearie?"

"Two autumn spice coffees and two pumpkin muffins."

Julia had been good to me, and I wanted to thank her, so I took off early—Taylor didn't question why I wanted to leave an hour ahead of schedule—before the coffee shop closed its doors. With goodies in hand, I trekked a half mile downtown to the clinic where she always remained after hours for our sessions.

Mrs. Robinson, the receptionist at the front, was leaving when I stepped inside. "Oh! Lyle, didn't you get the message?"

"What message?"

"Doctor Bearheart had me call the shop to reschedule, but you weren't there."

I showed off the carton holding our hot drinks and tasty treats. "I left early to get these."

"Oh! Well, she's not feeling so well today, so maybe a visit from you is just what she needs. She's still inside. Go on. Maybe you can convince her to rest and take a break from her computer too."

"Sure." I smiled at Mrs. Robinson and continued inside.

The smell hit me like a sucker punch in the gut before I crossed the lobby. I'd caught a faint trace of it while on the sidewalk, but the pure, concentrated scent of a shifter in heat took me by surprise. Behind me, the distant sound of the door clicking into the locked position as Mrs. Robinson left sounded like a gunshot.

Canceled appointment. It made sense to me a few seconds too late.

"Doctor Bearheart?" I called out in a hoarse whisper. I tried not to breathe through my nose, but I could practically taste her arousal in the air.

Fuck.

Proceeding with caution, I stepped into the hall and peered around the corner toward her office. The light shone through the open doorway, and I chose to face temptation head on to deliver her treats. I found her behind the desk, slumped back with an ice pack over her brow.

"Sorry, Lyle. I sent a message to postpone."

"Yeah. Mrs. Robinson said you canceled, but I didn't get the message." I frowned and studied her from across the room. "I just wanted to, ah, to bring this for you. I'll get out of your hair."

I tried to focus on coffee instead of the sexually-aroused woman in front of me with dilated, golden brown eyes blown so wide only a sliver of color remained around her pupils. Gently, I set the container on the counter beside me, struggling to ignore the tension growing in my jeans. She licked her lips, and my cock jumped.

"We can still…talk if you'd like," she replied as she abandoned her seat to move around her desk.

Was it my imagination, or did her gaze drop to my crotch when she said that?

"I really appreciate the snacks." Appreciated them so much she didn't even give them a glance and drifted closer to me.

It really hit me then, a smack of pheromones straight to the face, making my dick stand at attention. She didn't have her lab coat on for once, and her blouse was unbuttoned enough to show a teasing peek of black lace beneath the cobalt silk. She'd kicked her heels off somewhere, now barefoot, standing just an inch or two shorter than me without the sexy shoes.

"I'll just. Uh." On the next breath, my dick pulsed with need, and all I could imagine was hiking her skirt around her hips.

Those fantasies were nothing new. Too many times I'd imagined her lips against mine, pliant and yielding, breasts crushed against my chest. I'd wanted to take her in my arms for the past month of our appointments together, but I'd been careful never to violate our doctor and patient relationship.

Ian had warned me about that, pointing out Jules had enough on her mind. Fuck. When did she become Jules to me?

I tried not to breathe her in, but it was impossible. She was so close, her breath feathering against my chest. Julia was literally a bitch in heat, the first time in my life I'd ever encountered one.

"You should go," she whispered, but there was no insistence behind her words. Only her "come fuck me" eyes and her irresistible scent.

It was just her and me, the office empty, the doors locked behind us, and damn I wanted her.

"Is that what you really want?" I asked, suddenly confident. Cocky.

She was silent so long I started to wonder if I'd made a mistake. Read her wrong. Invented an interest where there was none, and this sensual act from her was hormones and nothing else.

"No," she finally said. "No, it's not what I want. What I want is to stop resisting you."

One kiss. Just one kiss and I'd leave, content with

the knowledge that I wasn't a coward and had finally acted on my desires. I only had one arm to hold her, and I used it to drag her close by the waist.

Then she was mine, her face tilting up to meet my lips. I claimed her thoroughly, tasting the sweetness of her tongue, shamelessly stroking in a slick dance. Just one kiss. Except once it began, I couldn't let her go. She rolled her hips, grinding against my dick while her palm cupped the back of my head and anchored me in place.

"Fuck," I breathed.

One kiss wasn't enough. My lips trailed to that ridge of bone exposed by her blouse and nibbled. Even her skin tasted sweet.

Her hands slid down both my arms without shying from my injury, nostrils flaring as she dragged my shirt up my chest and pulled it over my head. I didn't stop her.

We crashed against her desk and I hefted her up with one hand, setting her down on the bare, hard surface. When I couldn't find the zipper to her skirt, I growled and shoved it up around her hips instead.

"If you really want this, get my belt off."

Her agile fingers made quick work of the buckle and my zipper. "Done." She had the denim pushed down around my thighs before I could rip her panties off.

Patience was usually a virtue for me, but not now, not when she was writhing against me with her tight skirt hiked up around her waist. Wet, bare skin greeted my seeking fingers, and I groaned as she took me in her hand. She pumped once, then twice, gliding her hand up and down in this firm grip that drove me crazy with desire.

The desk behind her, neat and tidy with only her laptop and a couple of manila folders with my name scrawled across the tab, became the ideal place to claim my little coyote.

"Lay back."

Her hair fanned across the wood and fell over the desk edge. Looking at her sprawled out in front of me, still in her thigh high stockings, made me wonder how the hell I got so lucky. All this time I wanted her, and she'd wanted me, too.

Resisting the temptation to dive inside her, I pressed my thumb against her clit, rubbing gently while holding eye contact. I hadn't slept with a woman in years. A little more than three years, to be exact. She was hot and responsive, her breath catching in her throat when I teased two fingers between her swollen lips.

"Sweet Jesus, you're so wet."

I'd never forgive myself if I didn't at least taste her.

I dipped down and drew in a deep breath, my nose against the soft, dark curls groomed into a neat triangle. Then my tongue lapped where my finger had been just seconds before, a teasing taste while I twisted my hand and rubbed my two fingers against her inner flesh. Her scent washed over me.

If ever a time came where I wished I still had both

hands, it was now. But I made do with what I had, gliding the same two fingers until they disappeared to the knuckle. She moaned a sound of pure heaven to my ears, and I throbbed with the urgent need to take her and make a claim over the little wild coyote. Her thighs tensed, trembling with the next tongue stroke. I didn't know yet if this would be the only time, but I knew I'd do anything I could to convince her we deserved more.

12

JULIA

*M*y fingers tightened in his hair, my mind conflicted. Part of me wanted to reverse our positions, the other part wanted to keep his face and talented tongue where they belonged. His rough padded fingers gave the perfect friction, stroking inside me while his tongue curled around my clit.

"Lyle—fuck!"

He moved his hand in quick strokes, and my mind blanked, pressure and pleasure building within me. Faster and faster, his fingers slid in and out too quick for me to follow, pushing within my soaked channel until orgasm overtook me and I spasmed against the desk. Pens clattered against the floor, and my head knocked against my closed laptop.

Apparently, he could use his tongue for more than fast talking customers into purchases at the shop.

My need for Lyle was like a wild brushfire blazing

out of control, one orgasm barely enough to quench the reckless flames within me. I groaned, reduced to a wanton and desperate state beneath him, loathing the loss of his mouth but craving him inside my body.

He fumbled for a minute with his jeans and wallet then pulled out a thin foil packet. I found enough strength to sit up and help with the condom, rolling it down his rigid shaft. He was so thick that when he straightened to align the crown against my entrance, I had doubts about whether he'd fit.

"You have no idea how long I been wantin' you, Jules."

Jules. It was always ma'am with him, with that adorable, southern accent.

He rolled the tip up and down, gathering slickness on the condom before pressing between my folds. He slipped in, feeding one inch after the next.

"Unfasten your blouse for me, baby."

Buttons. So many damn buttons. After the first two, I gave a frustrated groan and popped the rest. The silk parted and left me with only my lace bralette. Lyle didn't seem to mind my meager proportions, drinking me in with his eyes, and I saw the moment when his matching desire took hold of him. He bucked forward, sinking full girth within. And it felt damned fine, the delicious stretch making my body burn and tingle, delighting in the painful edge to the pleasure.

"Damn, I've wanted this too," I panted, losing all inhibitions. "Say it again, Lyle. Call me Jules." I wriggled on the desk, scooting a little closer to the edge.

Then I leaned up to meet him halfway for a heated kiss while I shrugged my blouse off and cast it aside.

"My Jules," he grunted out on the next thrust, bucking inside me again.

Thrilled by his claim, my body became abuzz with sensation in all the right places. I clenched around him. Hormones and endorphins scorched through me, dulling all common sense and shattering my ability to separate right from wrong.

He was my patient. My patient who had become the most well-endowed lover I'd ever had, beginning a blissful, slow rhythm with distinct thrusts, each stroke gliding the full length of him to completion. After yanking down my bralette, he squeezed my breast and scraped his coarse thumb over the tensed nipple, rasping it with calloused skin.

"I want you to be mine."

His. The words went through me like a shock, and in that moment, I wanted nothing more than to be his. To have his scent all over me. Inside me. *Permanently* part of me.

"Too slow," I moaned against his mouth. "I need you. All of you."

He bucked his hips, picking up the pace, and gave my nipple a small twist. "Like that, baby? Tell me what you want, Jules."

"You! Fuck, Lyle. I want…harder." I asked and he gave, words silenced as we both groaned and huffed, bodies slapping together hard and fast. The desk jostled beneath us, sliding across the floor each time he slammed home.

Trying to deny my attraction to him had been an exercise in futility. In pain. An impossible thought flit through my mind—could he be my forever mate, that rare and magical bond that occurred at times between shifters destined to be together?

I tried not to think about it, but it crept into my mind again, along with the yearning to feel him balls deep inside me, his powerful body behind mine. As each slam drove me closer to the edge, I admired the lean vision above me, in awe of his straining muscles and how they flexed and glistened beneath the fluorescent office lights. I could have watched his abs all night.

"This how you like it?" He turned his head and laved his tongue over the tip of my breast, sucking the nipple between his lips while his fingers played with the other.

It sent a little zip right to my core, making my thighs tremble and shake around him. My answer was lost in a second shudder of my entire body, driven to orgasm by an angled stroke that bumped his tip against my sweet spot. He churned through the resistance to prolong my pleasure.

"Oh God, don't stop. Don't stop, Lyle," I moaned. My toes curled tight, and my heels pressed into his muscled ass.

"No way I'm stopping, baby." He lost control, pushing faster and faster, gripping my leg with a bruising hold.

Good. I wanted them. I wanted him to mark me in every way possible.

Wet sounds of skin slapping against skin filled the small office. Despite his promises, he stiffened atop me and threw back his head, gorgeous brown eyes shut as the muscles in his shoulders and neck went taut. The sound of my name from his lips sounded closer to a vocalization of victory than a moan, each noise wrapped in a guttural growl.

Yes!

All the while I clenched around his throbbing length, milking him for the hot burst my excited body craved. Every inch of me was sensitive and trained on him, eager for his touch and kisses, flushed with desire.

He nuzzled my breast afterward while recovering his breath, his brow slick against my skin. "Fuck, girl."

As we lay there, catching our breaths, I stroked my fingers down his dampened back. He didn't withdraw immediately, still hard after climax.

I loved dog shifters. Their erections always endured for a while after they were spent for the last drop. A few aftershocks danced along his dick, prompting him to make a quiet, appreciative groan.

Eventually when he did soften, his withdrawal left me feeling lost. Empty.

"Hey, Jules… We got a slight problem." I opened my eyes to glance toward his voice to see my nude Adonis standing beside the desk with a blown condom between his fingers. "I think it was too old."

"It's fine," I mumbled.

He blinked at me. "Really?"

"I have an implant." And an insatiable craving for more of him. "It'll be fine."

His eyes lit up with interest. "Yeah?"

Without concern for the consequences or my disheveled clothes, I slid off the desk and shoved him down into my chair so I could straddle his hips. "I hope you're ready to go again, because I can't wait."

And since I was going to hell for breaking my code, I might as well get everything I wanted while I could. Because tomorrow… Tomorrow I had to be his doctor again.

13

JULIA

*T*hanks to the IUD I'd had placed four years ago, I didn't worry too much about the broken condom. Access to Lyle's medical records had told me weeks ago he was clean as a whistle. I'd had him tested for everything at the onset. No STDs tied to that delicious body. He'd made love to me like some kind of sexual god for most of the evening, sating my mating urgency for the first time since the cycles began during my teen years.

Afterward, we cuddled in my office chair until it was long after dark, reluctant to part despite the waning evening. But I knew the longer I held him, the less likely I'd want to let go. The more I'd want to keep him for myself and run my fingers through his red hair if it meant he'd always look at me with those love-struck, adoring eyes.

He didn't let me drop him off at home, swearing he enjoyed the walk because it gave him time to think. So

I drove across the tracks and to the city limits by myself with a cup of microwaved seasonal coffee and a pumpkin muffin. I wolfed down the latter and guzzled the coffee before I reached Ian's driveway. I had to fasten my lab coat over my ruined blouse just in case I crossed paths with him or Leigh.

When I finally dragged myself from bed before lunch, I was happy to sequester myself in Ian's cozy living room with a book I'd been meaning to read but never had the time to enjoy.

Thankfully, my eagle friend wasn't remotely interested in my smell. If he noticed anything amiss at all, he didn't utter a word.

"Tea?" Leigh asked.

I looked up from my book and blinked at her smiling features. She held two steaming mugs decorated with American bald eagles.

"Thanks, though I'm not sure I need the caffeine this late in the afternoon."

Leigh chuckled and took a seat beside me. "Don't worry, it's herbal. I made a big pot of this stuff some pushy clerk pressed on me at the mall yesterday. It's supposed to be like cinnamon almond caramel or something."

After accepting her kind offer, I breathed in the steam but neither it nor my book got Lyle off my mind. "Thanks."

It was foolish. Irresponsible. Unprofessional.

"Everything all right?" Leigh asked.

I'd be in so much trouble if anyone found out.

"Yeah, why?"

"Well, I noticed that you're still on the same chapter title page now as you were about twenty minutes ago when I passed through the room. You seem sort of distracted."

For an ordinary human, Leigh perceived as much as any shifter. I set my book aside and twisted on the couch until I was facing her, tucking my feet up.

"How did you know Ian was the right guy for you? I mean, were you daunted by his age at all?"

"Well, he came after me, and I pushed him away a bit because I didn't want charity. We were only friends, then I got into legal issues with Sophia's grandparents, and Ian flew to my rescue." Her blue eyes twinkled when she spoke.

"That's Ian." I sighed. "He's like Clark Kent without the glasses."

"That would make him Superman," Leigh said, ducking out of the way of my swat. "So to be honest with you, yes, I was worried he was too old for me at first. But Betty told me he's been gray since his twenties, and he doesn't look his age or act it."

"Except for when he's pulling rank," I muttered.

Leigh laughed. "Well, yeah, only then. He does it with me sometimes until I tell him where he can shove his 'advice,' and he remembers he's not *my* colonel."

I chuckled with her.

"Is there some older guy you're involved with?"

No. One younger. My thirty-seven to Lyle's twenty-eight felt like robbing a nursery.

I shook my head. "No."

"One younger?" Leigh asked, more astute than I'd anticipated.

I didn't reply.

"Is it Lyle?"

Get out. My mortified expression must have told her everything, because her eyes lit up and her mouth fell open.

Somehow, I didn't fumble my cup when she cried out, "It's Lyle!"

"What makes you jump to that conclusion?" I asked and carefully, deliberately sipped my tea.

"Well, you two have been spending a lot of time together."

"Right. At the clinic. For appointments." I took another sip to cover my unease.

"And then there's that time last week when I was pushing Sophia on the swing at the park, and you were working rehab stuff with him and he just kept giving you these puppy dog eyes. You know, sort of how Petunia looks at Ian when he's offering her peanut butter in the kitchen behind my back and thinks I can't see him."

Did he? Sifting back through my thoughts and memories, I supposed she was right. I always ignored it. Or tried to.

"He looks good, too," Leigh commented. "I mean, now that he's off drugs and stuff."

"And a muscled machine." I sighed. "I guess that's new because of prison?"

Leigh shook her head. "Well, yeah. And no. We went to high school together, and he was always sort of cute before, especially for a ginger, but his habits and attitude turned me off. Then he put on some weight after school while smoking dope all the time and sitting around Tito's place."

"He's really done better for himself, hasn't he?"

"He sure has. I like this Lyle a lot more." Leigh's smile widened, and she poked me in the ribs. "Just not as much as you do."

No matter how much I wanted to deny it, I couldn't. "Don't tell Ian. Please."

"What? Girl, please." Leigh waved it off. "You don't have to worry about me saying a word to him. He'll figure that out on his own, if he hasn't already." She leaned forward, and a big grin spread across her face. "Because you look at Lyle the same way he looks at you."

~

Thanks to some government pull and greasing a few hands, I had gained admitting privileges at a local hospital to perform an inpatient procedure. All expenses came out of our program budget, and the operating room staff underwent a strict approval process before they signed their individual nondisclosure agreements.

Three days after our romp, Ian drove Lyle to the hospital. I'd arrived hours ahead of his scheduled operation to coach the surgical staff a second time about my expectations and their role.

I couldn't help but regret the days of isolation from him. In a way, I'd failed him as his doctor and a friend. What if he was afraid? Part of my duty also involved soothing his concerns, and I couldn't do that while avoiding him because sex-starved Mother Nature decided to rear her head and seduce him. I knew if I saw him again the next day, or even the day after, I'd have him again and again until I lost count of the ways I made him growl "Jules."

After gulping down coffee in the OR staff lounge, I moved into the clean corridors connecting the surgical rooms to the pre-op and recovery rooms. Annie, the nurse assigned to deliver his personal care during the procedure and afterward, smiled as I approached her.

"He's prepped," she told me. "The CNRA will be in soon to chat with him about the anesthesia."

"Great. I'm going to go have a word with him before the procedure. Did he sign the consents?"

"Every one of them, Doctor Bearheart."

"Great."

I traveled to the room where Lyle awaited me on a narrow hospital bed. He wore a standard gown and lay beneath a blanket tugged up to his chest.

"Good morning, Jules," Ian greeted me.

"Mornin'," Lyle murmured.

Those puppy dog eyes drank me in, and I smiled back at him despite the fluttering in my chest. Whenever I saw him, my heart picked up a skipping rhythm, and my fingers ached to touch his flushed cheeks.

"Good morning, you two. Are you ready to get down with this thing?" I asked Lyle as I moved up to the bedside. I set one hand on his shin above the blanket and electricity leapt between us. With Ian present, I didn't dare to do anything more.

"I'm about as ready as I'll ever be," Lyle said. He gave me a weak grin. "I'm excited but...I've never had a surgery before until that gator took my arm, you know?"

"You'll be in good hands," Ian assured him. "You won't find better than Julia."

"Except for Doctor Vogt, right?" Lyle asked, referring to Sasha.

I smiled. "I'll fight her for the title of best doctor. Anyway, do you have any last minute questions or concerns?"

Lyle shook his head. "No. Just glad you're here."

I wished Ian would flutter away somewhere else to grant us a few moments of privacy, but Lyle's uncertain, shy smile flustered me too much to create a valid excuse for kicking him out.

"Well then, I'll see you once you're awake."

After flashing him another smile, I exited the room and went to count my tools a second time. Menial tasks grounded me back to reality and dragged my focus back to where it belonged.

By the time they wheeled Lyle into the OR, I was ready.

Today, both of our dreams would come true.

Nearly eleven hours passed in surgery to reopen the old injury, remove atrophied tissue, graft the bone and metal, and reattach old nerves with fine stitches. Charles and Lyle's wounds weren't identical, but they were close.

And Lyle had already given me permission to remove more if necessary. By the time we were finished, the medical staff gazed at me with awestruck eyes. I'd answered their questions plainly during the procedure, explaining it was a prototype we hoped to provide to our veterans in the future if his body didn't reject it. If it didn't cause him more pain than it was worth. So many ifs.

Exhaustion weighed me down, but I pushed it aside and took a seat beside his bed in the recovery room. I didn't want him to wake up alone in an unfamiliar place, hurting.

I wanted to be the first face he saw when he woke up.

"Nngh..." he moaned quietly, cheek turned against a white pillow. "Jules."

"I'm right here." I settled my hand over his and stroked his knuckles. "Take it easy, big guy. You're pumped up on some good medicines, and you'll be a little disoriented."

Another peek up at his monitors showed the same thing they had the last thirty times—strong vitals. After a few more minutes, his eyes blinked open, groggy and unfocused. That didn't last long. He zoomed in on my face and managed a faint, lopsided smile.

Then he was out again.

He drifted in and out of sleep for another fifteen minutes before he finally spoke in more than an incoherent mumble.

"Hey, beautiful. Did it work?"

Beautiful. He called me beautiful. I smiled at him with tears in my eyes, though I quickly blinked them away and leaned over his bed to draw the white sheets and hospital blanket higher over his chest. "We'll find out once you're healed. How do you feel?"

"Tired. You're kinda blurry," he answered, only to conclude after a brief pause, "Still pretty though."

A deep, masculine cough came from behind me, and I whirled to see Ian standing beyond the open doorway beside Taylor.

"We come at a bad time? We had to bribe people to get back here," the cougar joked.

"He's just waking up, and he's pretty loopy," I replied, straightening my lab coat. "Come on in. I'm sure he won't mind some visitors. Would you, Lyle?"

He rolled his head on the pillow and looked over. "Hey, guys… Come to stare at—well, I haven't even looked yet." He laughed, which turned into a cough, so I stepped over with a cup of melting ice chips and a straw.

"Hey, this brings back memories," Taylor said, grinning down at Lyle from the foot of the hospital bed.

The dog shifter sucked thirstily from the straw and raised his middle finger at my friends. They laughed.

"Slow sips," I cautioned.

"Contrary to Taylor's insensitive joking, we're glad to see you're doing good. I brought cards from the kids," Ian said.

Everybody knew it was a big day for him. Lyle had told the kids he would get fitted with some new prosthetic but wasn't allowed to say more about it.

"Would you like to have a look?" I asked Lyle. "Or do you want to wait?"

"I'll wait. Doubt I'd be able to read them right now. I'm so... Man. What did they give me?"

"Dilaudid, and you'll have plenty of time to read them later," I told him. "You'll stay here for a few days until we're confident everything is healing well, then you'll enjoy some bed rest back home."

"Mama's gonna make such a fuss," he whined, earning smiles from all three of us.

"Aw, man, let her," Taylor said.

I retreated to a chair closer to the window, distancing myself so Lyle could focus on Ian and Taylor, but the old eagle followed me.

"You know, your part in this is over," Ian said, grinning at me with this knowing, cocksure look, as if he knew more than he should. "You should probably get some rest, Jules."

I grunted and feigned interest in my cell phone. "He's my patient, Ian. What kind of doctor would I be if I didn't have an interest in his welfare?"

Ian snorted, but said nothing else. To me at least. He took a seat at the foot of Lyle's bed and looked him over. "You're a brave man for doing this. I just wanted you to know that."

"Being her guinea pig? Nah… It's not like I have anything to lose. Y'all save the compliments for when these drugs wear off and I start to have regrets."

I gave him a worried glance. About a week ago, Lyle had expressed concerns about getting addicted to opiates again. I promised not to let that happen.

"We should let him rest. I'll be back to check in on you in the morning, but I think I'll grab a few hours of shut-eye myself." Ian had that much right, at least. I was exhausted. "Do you want me to bring you anything? Or are you going to brave the hospital food?"

"Just wanna sleep," Lyle muttered. He was gone again before we even reached the hallway.

I tugged the door shut behind us. "What?"

Ian was eyeballing me, though Taylor appeared oblivious. Disinterested. Maybe *too* much so. He made an excuse to go grab some coffee, leaving Ian and me alone in the hallway.

So I sighed and dragged a hand through my hair. "Spit it out, whatever you have to say."

With his hands in his pockets, Ian glanced up and down the halls. "Well. It's probably none of my business."

"Which has never stopped you from giving your advice in the past," I said, voice dry.

He chuckled and shrugged. "You know me well.

Anyway, I'm just concerned about you. You're cutting it a little close, don't you think?"

"Cutting what close?" I crossed my arms over my chest and stared him down. "We've followed the timetable for Lyle's replacement exactly."

"I'm not referring to the timetable for his replacement, and you know it. You'll have him ready by Christmas as projected by the plans. I'm asking if there's something going on between you two."

"That wouldn't be any of your business," I told him. "I'm his doctor, Ian. That's… It would be unprofessional of me for there to be anything else." But was I trying to convince him or myself?

"Doesn't take a genius to see that boy cares about you, Jules. I'm just tryin' to look out for him."

A quick glance up and down the hall ensured we were alone. Or as alone as we could be in a hospital. I lowered my voice though. "Look, he's a great guy, and I'm not a cold-hearted bitch out to hurt him, but this… It's complicated."

He crossed his arms and stared me down in return, resembling my dad more than an old friend and former squad leader. "I've been watching him give you puppy eyes for the past two weeks. It's more than complicated at this point."

Dammit. First Leigh and now Ian? I muttered uncomplimentary things under my breath. "Look, I messed up, okay? I'm trying to figure out how to fix it. So back off and stop playing the father card."

Ian held up both hands in surrender. "I'm not trying

to be your dad, Julia, but some things can't be stuffed back into Pandora's Box." He glanced at the door between us, his brows wrinkled, and he frowned deeply before saying, "I'm not judging you, either. He's not the same guy we busted back then. Maybe this is what both of you need."

"I know that. I judged him unfairly, and I've admitted that much. He's not a bad guy. It's just…"

Who was I kidding? Lyle wasn't a bad guy; he was a wonderful guy with the best qualities any woman could desire in a mate—loyal, brave, kind, dependable, and honest.

I shook my head and moved off down the hall, Ian trailing beside me. "Like I said, I'm his doctor. And until this whole thing is done, it's gonna have to stay that way." Even though I wanted to pick up where we'd left off, taking him for another wild ride, this time without my inner coyote urging it to happen.

"All I'm saying is, with the holidays around the corner, it'd be nice if you had a family to spend it with."

My brother's widow and I had a tepid relationship, and she'd be spending the holiday with her relatives as usual. I'd sent gifts for the kids a couple weeks ago and didn't expect a thank you note in return.

"You're my family now."

"And I'm very honored to have you in my home for Christmas, but I can think of others who need you more."

"Thanks, *Dad*."

Ian sighed. "All right. Forget I said anything. You're an adult, and you're free to make your own decisions."

If anything, I'd expected Ian to chastise me for mixing business with pleasure, not encourage me to be selfish.

What happened with Lyle should never have occurred, but it did, and I was half convinced my shifter hormones were responsible.

"So, how long until he's on his feet again and able to use it?"

"If he were a normal man, he'd be here for weeks. But we all heal quickly, so I'll give him a few days before he can head home. I'll be doing a few baseline tests with him tomorrow, and you're welcome to come watch if you'd like. He might enjoy having a cheering squad."

He chuckled. "Sure thing. I'll swing by."

Taylor reappeared with our coffees and passed a cup into my hand.

I walked with the guys down to the parking lot and suffered through veiled insinuations as they gave each other knowing looks. I wasn't fooling myself, and I sure couldn't fool them.

14

LYLE

*T*he four days in the hospital never gave us any time alone. There was always a nurse in the room or some intern doctor in-the-know about us. He smelled like a reptile of some sort. Maybe a snake. I hated snakes. But I only saw Jules a few times in and out because she had decided not to tax me too soon.

Then it was off home, where Mama fussed over me like I was a toddler again. She'd cleaned out the office and made it a proper bedroom, claiming my 'nice friends' had helped with the heavy lifting. I guessed that meant Taylor and Ian. Russ, too, judging from all the fixed up woodwork. Why they bothered with me I still didn't know, but I had to admit it was nice to sleep in a real fucking bed and not on a lumpy, ancient couch.

Healing of the surgical site progressed as normal, the bone gradually bonding to whatever she'd installed in me. I had trouble describing the sensations to her, like a blanket of pain wrapped around my stump, each point of agony impossible to differentiate from the last. Although I couldn't feel the forearm itself, I felt the raw, open wound she'd made to connect the prosthetic to my body.

My new arm wasn't useful for anything yet, just a lot of dead weight in a sling. Pretty dead weight though, sleek and matte black like a thing out of a science fiction movie. Julia had promised she was working on a synthetic skin covering so I wouldn't always draw attention, but I kind of liked it. I couldn't stop looking at it and wondering how it would feel to have sensation in my fingers again.

She hadn't lied when she said it would hurt, that there were times I'd want to quit, but we were beyond that point now and in a whole new league. There'd be no removing this thing unless it was killing me.

With that grim thought in mind, I wondered if it would. If I'd made the mother of all fuckups by inviting this thing into my life.

Nah. Because accepting it had brought Jules to me. I'd rather die and take those memories with me than return to the loneliness I had before.

There were moments of pain so excruciating I shook, but I kept those from Mama. At first, I'd even tried to hide it from Julia, too, not that it had a chance in hell of working. She saw right through it, forced me to take a Tramadol, and tucked me into bed again. Then she tattled on me, told Mama to stick to the pain

guideline she'd drawn out, and to call her back if I
didn't take my meds.

By the weekend, I was more than ready to head out
to the clinic, nervous and anxious as all hell. Not just
about my arm, but seeing her again. It seemed like a
dream now. She'd only dropped in once a day to check
on me at home.

After the way she treated me in the hospital, I was
half-convinced I'd hallucinated the evening in her
office anyway. Maybe I did.

With an afternoon appointment to see her in the
office, I idled around Mama's house then checked the
time. I had an hour before I was due to see Julia, and
for the first time in days, I felt one hundred percent
pain free. Eager to check in on Kevin and see if his
outlook about ratting out Jed had changed, I laced up
my boots and made my way out into the brisk
November weather.

We'd be in hoodies and jackets soon, though there
were some Texans out there wearing their flip-flops
into December.

"Good afternoon there, Lyle!" Mr. Webber called.

"Hi, Mr. Webber. How ya doin'?" Before I could
make it past his gate, the old man had left his seat on
the porch and picked his way down to the fence.
Without looking at my watch, I smiled back at him.

"Just fine. It's a wonderful day out today, isn't it?"
His attention dropped to the blue sling supporting my
glossy, metallic new arm. It gleamed like a new penny
in shades of black and gunmetal gray. "Your mother

told us you'd had surgery, but I never expected to see anything like this. How are you feelin', son? We just didn't think you'd be on your feet again so soon."

"First day I've felt like me again," I admitted, startled by his concern. "I guess I heal fast."

His eyes twinkled. "I suppose you do. If you or Peggy need anything, you be sure to let us know."

After I found my voice again, I promised him we'd do just that and continued on my way. The support and caring of other people in the community always took me by surprise. I'd become accustomed to wallowing in bitterness and believing they looked down on me.

Kevin's family lived on an isolated patch of land without any immediate neighbors. After traveling about five minutes down the dirt road past my street, I made a left and continued on a dusty, pebbled path shaded by dense forest to the left. The other side of the road was open pasture filled with about three or four dozen of the Wilson family's grazing cattle. I didn't know much about farming and all that junk, but their business didn't seem to do much more than float them at the poverty line.

I also didn't know Mark Wilson well, but I'd crossed paths with him recently at Quickdraw's feed store when fetching pellets for the chickens. He struck me as a self-righteous asshole of the highest caliber who couldn't be bothered to return my hello when we were standing in the checkout lane.

If he treated Kevin the same way, no wonder the boy did anything he could to get his father's attention. I shook my head and crossed the short-trimmed yard, passing a broke down Chevy sedan covered in a layer of fall leaves. It hadn't moved in a long while.

The thing about old trailer houses is that their walls are paper-thin sheets with little insulation. Before I reached the bottom step of the porch, a panicked wail preceded the sharp crack of skin against skin.

"He's just a boy, Mark! Stop!"

"Bitch, you say another word, and this'll be your ass-beating too!"

Another slap rang out, a boy's cry, the meaty thump of a fist on a soft body. Instincts took over, and my feet pounded up the steps. When the knob didn't turn in my hand, my right shoulder did the work. I crashed it into the door with all my strength. The frame yielded like old plywood, and the door swung open with a bang when it rebounded off the wall.

Mark Wilson stood over his wife with a belt in his hand while their son lay stretched over the ground sobbing and retching, holding his gut. A fresh shiner had swollen his left eye shut.

Although Hillary Wilson was of a darker complexion, a smooth brown shade like nutmeg, red welts and whip marks stood out against her legs.

Screw this dude. Trembling with rage, I barged in.

"Who the fuck are you coming in this house?" Mark demanded. "This is private property, boy, and you'd better get the hell out before I get my gun."

I didn't give a damn about trespassing in his house, or the gun he didn't have on his body right now. "You wanna hit somebody? Come and hit me, then. You such a man you can hit on women and kids."

"This boy? This ain't a kid. This little troublemaker ain't even mine, and he oughta be damned glad he got a place to sleep at night."

With a few words of spewed trash, Mark elevated my temper to nuclear levels. I lurched forward toward him, seeing only red and dangerously close to shifting in my clothes, because never in my life had I ever wanted to maul someone into a pile of wet tissue and bone than I did this guy.

We went after each other at the same time, both of us with something to prove. As I weaved to the side, Mark's fist struck the space previously occupied by my chin. With my left arm in a sling he must have thought he'd have the advantage.

But man, I aimed to prove him wrong and fuck his world up, because he'd messed with the wrong kid. Hurt the wrong woman. Hillary was a nice lady, and now all those times I'd seen her in aviator shades made sense.

My right fist crashed into Mark's nose. Blood erupted from it, spilling down his face. My next punch landed in his gut, folding him like a house of cards. I didn't need two hands to mess him up, even if I hadn't been blessed with superhuman, shifter reflexes.

Lacking even an ounce of guilt for using my natural gift, I caught the back of his head and brought his face down into my right knee. The fight was over before it started. I dropped him like a stone and stepped back.

"Come on. You're such a big man. Wasn't you gonna beat the shit out of me too? Or does that only apply to women and teenage boys? I got one arm working here, man. C'mon and whoop me down too."

With blood pouring over his mustached upper lip and down his chin, Mark pushed himself up on his elbows. Neither his wife nor his son went to his side. They were huddled together on the floor, as if they'd been there a thousand times before under this bastard's foot.

"You better get gone, you asshole, before I call the cops. You're trespassin' and this ain't any of your damn business."

"Go ahead and call. Tell 'em a man with one arm beat your ass and said he'd do it again. Let me hear one fucking word about you laying hands on this woman or boy after this, and I won't blink about earning my way back to prison. It'll be worth it."

Mark pushed himself up off the floor and mopped his bloody face with his shirt. He hauled ass to the door and snatched his car keys off the hook beside it. "This shit ain't over if you think I'm gonna let some strung-out junkie run me out of my home. Just you wait."

He ran down to his truck, started the engine, and peeled out onto the road like the devil was on his tail. I would have grinned if there was anything else to laugh about.

I turned to see Hillary helping Kevin up from the ground. The days of missed school made sense, and I wondered how many times the system had failed him.

Someone should have looked into his home life. Seen this shit. Helped him and Hillary out of this bind before it came down to me having to intervene by luck.

"Y'all okay?"

"I think so," Kevin said shakily.

"Hillary, I don't think it's safe to stay here. If that man comes back, there's no telling if he'll have a weapon or go for his gun. You gotta get out."

"I don't have anywhere to go… My mother lives hours away in Dallas. My car won't move. Mark's been promising for months to get it fixed for me."

"Then we'll get it moving."

It took me five minutes to determine it was the alternator, not even a difficult part to replace. She needed new tires, one of them flatter than pizza and another with a huge bulge waiting to rupture at the wrong place and wrong time while she was driving.

"Can I use your phone?"

She was hovering over her son with a cool slab of meat for his face. "Sure, sure," she murmured, distracted.

I made a call to Taylor's shop, and without mincing words, told him exactly what happened.

"She needs an alternator for a 2008 Chevy Aveo. I know it's a lot to ask but—"

"I'll be right there with the tow truck and a loaner. Tell Mrs. Wilson we got her covered."

Ten minutes later Taylor and Jada arrived in two vehicles. Jada headed inside to check on Hillary and

Kevin while I helped Taylor hitch her busted car onto his tow truck.

"Where's Mark?"

"Took off in his rig a couple minutes before I phoned you. He's got a gun in the trailer, but I didn't let him get to it."

"Good. Ian's on the way. He'll probably have a couple guys out to look for him."

I sat in the passenger seat of TJ's tow truck while we watched Jada, Hillary, and Kevin emerge a few minutes later with luggage and bags. His bruised face pissed me off all over again.

"You can take this all outta my pay—"

"Nah. No need for it to come out of your check, Lyle. I'm glad to help. Hell, I can write it off, probably. Charitable contribution or some shit," he said with a shrug, watching his wife through the windshield. "Jada says this happened a couple years ago. People saw Hillary with all kinds of bruises, but she swore a horse kicked her. That it wasn't Mark."

"I could have killed him, TJ."

"To be honest, I'm glad you didn't but kind of wish you did. Anyway, I doubt he'll have her to protect him this go around since you witnessed it all."

When Ian arrived, he took charge of the entire situation. He dismissed us both after I gave an account of what happened, from the moment of my arrival to the time Mark made his escape. Giving a statement about what I saw renewed my fury.

If I had a wife, or even a kid half as awesome as

Kevin, I'd give them the world. I'd work twice as hard at everything I did.

"Want me to drop you off at your street?" Taylor asked.

With a few measured breaths, I released the anger and brushed it aside because wishing death on Mark Wilson wasn't going to change what happened. "Nah. Supposed to be over to see Julia about my arm. Today's the day it comes out of the sling, and I'll finally be able to use two hands again."

Taylor dropped his gaze to my immobile left arm. At first, his brows drew together, then his eyes widened. He shook his head in disbelief. "I was so distracted with what was happening I didn't even realize… You jacked him up with just one arm, eh?"

"Yeah. I guess I did. I didn't really need two arms to do it."

Taylor grinned. "How many assholes did you have to mess up in prison? Be honest."

"Like three, dude. They didn't screw with me much after that."

"Ha. For me, it was four. God that stint sucked. Worst undercover job ever."

I snickered. "I heard about that while I was in. They turned you into a legend."

On the way back into town, we traded stories about our time in the penitentiary, his six months to discover the source of the drug ring in east Texas, and my three years for my involvement in it all.

Compared to Tito, my former boss, I got off light.

He'd be doing hard time for the next twenty-two years before he even touched parole.

Taylor pulled up alongside the clinic and let me out. Jada had turned a left at the intersection, taking Kevin and his mother down to the shop to wait for TJ.

"Hey," he called once I was out on the ground.

"What?"

"You did a real great thing. I just wanted to let you know that you might have saved their lives."

"Hell, man, Kevin's one of my kids. No one deserves that."

Giving him a wave, I pushed the door shut then stepped inside.

"Hello Lyle," Mrs. Robinson greeted me with a big smile at the reception counter. "Wow, would you look at that. Looks like something straight outta that movie with Arnold."

I looked down at the arm in the sling and chuckled. "Yes, ma'am, I guess it does look a bit like that." Minus the cables and rods at least, appearing sculpted from metal like a carbon copy of the original arm and hand with short, blunt fingernails sculpted at the end of each digit.

"Well, it looks good on you. Go on back."

She buzzed me through to the back of the clinic, and I ventured to Julia's office. She sat behind the desk, chewing one of her nails while staring at the laptop screen. She wore jeans and a colorful, autumn blouse in golden brown, red, and orange, her black hair accented by a single blue feather.

"Hey, doc."

"Hey. Grab a seat. This will just take me a minute to finish." She looked up and flashed me a quick smile, then went back to her laptop. Her fingers flew across the keyboard, and after a minute, she nudged it aside and stood. "How are you feeling? You look good and rested. I—is that blood on your shirt?" She stared at my jeans; there was more blood on my knee.

Shit.

"It's not mine!" I blurted out as she rushed to my side and raised her hands to my chest. "I got into a fight with a woman-beating jerk, and I guess he was too much of a dick to not bleed on me when he went down."

Concerned eyes raised to mine. "Who did you get in a fight with?"

"It was..." I sighed. "Ah hell, I guess you'll hear about it tonight since you're staying with Ian." Her brows raised, so I hurried on. "I caught Kevin's dad beating on him and his mom. So I beat him back."

There was no mistaking the smile on her face, the look of elation and pleasure when she gazed at me. Her busy hands paused at my ribs. "As much blood as there is, I wager you broke his nose. Good. You're not hurt, then?"

I hadn't done it for praise, but damn it felt good to have hers. "Nah. He didn't land a punch."

As Taylor had in the truck, she looked at me with admiration and respect. "Kevin and his mom?"

"Ian's got their statements, and Taylor is gonna fix

up her car or give her a loaner. Then they're headed to Dallas for a bit."

"I'm sure Ian will say it if he hasn't already, but that was a foolish thing to do. You could have been hurt. Still, it was also brave of you, and I'm glad you stepped in."

Seeming satisfied that I wasn't hiding an injury, her hands dropped away, and she stepped back.

"So do I get to have this sling off now so I can beat him with two hands next time?" I asked, forcing some humor into my voice.

"That depends. How does the surgical site feel? How do *you* feel? Is there any pain or discomfort? Any tenderness?"

"I feel like a million bucks now. I haven't taken anything today." Because deep down, I was afraid of getting hooked on the shit again. It was one habit I didn't want to pick back up. After pleading with Mama, I managed not to take a single pill yesterday.

"Nothing tugged or flared during your beat-down?"

"Nope." I grinned

"That's good to hear. I suppose if you're willing and ready, I'll deactivate the nerve blocker, and we can see how it feels. Sound good?"

"Hell yeah." As nervous as I was, excitement zipped through me. I wanted to move the fingers I only felt as phantoms. I wanted to take her pretty face between two hands. Touch her. Stroke her hair. I wanted to be whole, not just for me, but for her. Not that she'd shied from my missing arm.

Looking at her desk now brought back that rush of memories. Small traces of 'us' lingered in the tiny room, beneath the smell of Febreeze and tropical Fabuloso.

She removed the sling and walked her fingers down the new arm. Something shifted and clicked beneath her touch, and then sensation flooded my brain at once. Too much. It all surged down my nerves in a sizzling feedback loop, assaulting me with warmth and pressure, the heat of her fingertips, the pressure applied by them, and the cool current of the air conditioner vent over our heads.

I jumped back from her and hit the wall, but escaping contact didn't sever the connection between my brain and new limb. "Holy shit."

"Breathe, Lyle." Her panicked eyes searched my face. "I know it's a lot to take in. Just breathe deep, and if it's too much, I can turn it off and we can wait another day."

"No, no. It's okay. It'll just be the same tomorrow as it is now, right?"

She nodded. "Yes. Does it hurt?"

"A little." Flashes of pain ebbed up and down my forearm, beginning at the elbow where I was flesh and blood, then traveling to my fingertips. *Breathe. Just breathe*, I told myself, pressing my back against the wall and closing my eyes. I tried to ignore the pins and needles sensation and focus on the good parts. "I can feel the AC."

"Good. That's good." Her voice drew closer and

closer, as did her scent. "I'm going to make a tiny adjustment, all right? See if I can lower the sensations a little bit. But basically, right now, your mind and the nerves we connected to the arm are acclimating."

Her touch, I felt it. It was strange though, not like how I felt her on my other arm with skin to skin, but I felt the warmth in her fingers against the strange alloys. Pressure.

I moved the fingers—my fingers—and curled them into a loose fist.

"Now, this hand is stronger than the other. You won't be able to crush coal into a diamond like Superman, but you could give a karate master a run for his money if we lined some bricks up for you," she pointed out while making an adjustment beneath some small, inconspicuous panel. "Like we discussed, it's waterproof. The real test will come when you shift."

"When can I do that?"

"One thing at a time." Her laughter huffed across my upper arm, a feathery caress that made my dick hard in an instant. "If you can handle this for a few days, we'll do a shift. All right? But get acclimated with it this way first. Now, how does that feel? Better? Less pain?"

"I like it." I rotated my wrist and spread my fingers as she led me through a range of motions.

She tested each finger and made me resist the pressure of her own hands. I overpowered her with ease.

"Good, good. It's as strong as I expected." Satisfied,

she released my arm and moved to step away, but I dragged her back against me with my new arm.

"Oof."

Her surprised squeak made me grin. Certain I wasn't hurting her, I looked down into her face and wrapped my other arm around her as well.

"I've wanted to do this. To hold you with both arms. It's strange, there's sensation but it isn't the same. Not really."

It tugged slightly at the tender connection of flesh and metal, but it wasn't the screaming agony I'd expected. Shifters healed faster than humans, not instantaneously or overnight, but quickly enough that I was able to function.

"Lyle, we shouldn't be doing this."

And just like that, my elation popped, my smile dropping into a frown. "So it's like that, then."

Both of her hands pressed against my chest. I let go, and she returned to the seat behind her desk while I flexed my left arm and focused on the new, unfamiliar hand.

"I have a few dexterity tests I'd like you to perform."

"Are we not gonna talk about what happened at all?"

She took a deep breath, let it out slow, then leaned back in her seat. "All right, then. It was completely unprofessional of me to come on to you the way I did. I'm supposed to be here as your doctor, and if we were in a hospital and found out, I would have lost my job. Beyond that, I feel like I took advantage of you. You came in during a bad time. A time when, well, the animals in us took control. I should have been more careful. Instead, I abused your trust."

My heart sank, forming a cold, leaden ball in the pit of my stomach. It didn't mean a thing to her after all. The beast had taken over, and instinct had shoved all else to the wayside.

"Oh." Shrugging it off, I broke eye contact and focused on the window over her shoulder. Easier than meeting her eye and raging. "Let's get this finished, then."

After an hour of motor skills tests, and a request to take it easy on the new arm in the first days of its use, she let me go. She put on a distant facade that wasn't at all like the true Julia I'd come to know, then she dismissed me with a phony smile.

As I walked down the street, I veered toward the garage, thoughts spinning with restored confidence. Somehow, I'd have to show her we were more than a doctor and a patient. Because I'd be damned if that night hadn't meant something to us both.

She was being stubborn. I could deal with stubborn. Stubborn could be fixed.

All I needed to do was come up with a plan, and I did my best thinking while working. So I ambled into the garage and gave the guys a wave.

"Holy shit, man. That the arm they fixed you up with? Sweet," Luis said.

"How the hell is it attached to you?" T-Bone took

me by the arm like he was looking under the hood of a car. "What the hell? Are you Robocop now?"

I barked out a laugh and shook my head. "No, the rest of me is normal. The NDA won't let me talk too much about it, but look at this." I opened and closed my fist, then for fun, I flipped Luis off. He'd bet a hundred bucks that my new hand would be useless.

"Bad ass, dawg. Maybe TJ will let you under the hood of a car again," T-Bone said. "I heard you were jacking dudes up with one arm earlier, and came shining through like a real superhero."

I flushed with pleasure, unable to control the heat surging to my cheeks. "Yeah, I did."

I'd never received so much praise in a single day, in all my life.

Before they could interrogate me about what went down, Taylor popped into the storefront, wiping his hands off on a grease towel. "Damn. She cut you loose on the world already?"

"Yup."

Being around my friends chased away the gloom of Julia's rejection. We laughed and BS'd around between their jobs, and toward the end of the work day, Taylor disappeared in his truck to fetch some equipment. Or so I thought. He returned a half hour later hauling in cardboard boxes labeled Christmas supplies.

I groaned at him. "Dude, we ain't even past Thanksgiving yet."

"I'm not putting them up now," he said.

"Thank God."

"Gonna do it the day after Turkey Day."

I sighed.

"So, while we're on the subject of the holidays, what are you doing for Thanksgiving and Christmas?" Taylor asked.

"Not sure yet. Mama usually likes to go to the church dinner but, well, I've never really been comfortable there. Y'know? All those old ladies just frown at me. Better to let her go alone and not be scorned." If I went, they'd just exclude her, and that was the last thing I wanted. "Maybe I'll just kick back and enjoy a quiet evening."

"She's not cooking?"

I shook my head. "She was going to since I'm back at home, but I asked her not to do it. Too much for just the two of us."

"Come to my place, then. Russ and Ian are frying a couple turkeys. Daniela is baking, and I think Leigh and Jada are making all the sides. Julia already RSVP'd since she's got some personal shit keeping her here." He grinned.

I put on a poker face, refusing to show pleasure when he mentioned Julia's name. "Nah, I don't wanna crash your party, man."

"Hey, it ain't crashing if you're invited."

Despite our rough beginnings, I liked Taylor. Hell, I'd liked him back before I knew his true identity. Before he'd turned out to be a mole in our drug operation. At first, I'd resented him and his team for what they'd done, but time in jail had given me some much-needed clarity.

"You don't have to come to both if you don't want to, and if it makes you feel better," he said while coming over to close up my register, "you can bring a dish. Leigh is putting together some kind of gift game thing for Christmas, too."

"Okay, okay, okay. Damn. I'm convinced."

"Hey. Come out back with me for a second before you go home."

Taylor led the way out back where he'd built up a secured lot for the cars he was working on. He bought up old junkers and fixed them, or if they were too far gone, he stripped them for parts and sold the rest as scrap.

"By the way, the Wilsons got off okay. Kevin left this for you." He passed over a folded piece of paper. "He also apologized to me about the break-in, fessed up and told his mom all about it and how you helped him out then, too. Ian's probably already picked up Jed and taken him in now that they have a witness statement."

"Kev's a good kid. I knew he'd make the right choice eventually."

"Yeah, he is. I told Hillary when he turns sixteen in a couple months to send him by the garage. I'd give him your old job."

"Wait. What?"

Taylor gestured to the yard. "Pick one."

"I'm not followin', man."

Taylor laughed. "Pick one, Lyle. You fix it up, you

can keep it. Consider it an audition, I guess. If you can
handle one of these and get it in working condition, I'll
get you some real work hours on the clients' cars."

My mouth dropped open. "Nah. Nooo way, man." I
waited for the punchline to the joke, staring at him
before my gaze darted out over the field of junk. They
weren't all bad looking, nothing some love and dent-
hammering couldn't fix on the outside. With a little
TLC, I'd have a nice ride again. I had Mama sell my old
car to make ends meet while I was locked up. "You're
not messing with me?"

"Not messing with you." He clapped his hand
against the back of my shoulder. "Besides, I figure if
you really wanna test that arm out and see what it can
do, this is a great way. So take your pick. Whatever
you want."

I grinned and imagined getting under the hood
again. "Deal. How about…" I moved forward to have a
look, even though I knew the inventory by heart. "How
about that Charger?"

"Planning to make your own General Lee?" he
asked, raising his brows.

"Maybe." My mind ran wild with the vision of Julia
in the passenger seat, a native Daisy Duke with her
long black hair whipped by the wind while we sped
down Texas roadways. She'd look hot in tiny shorts.

"All right, man." He tossed me a set of keys from the
lockbox just inside the door, followed by a rag. "Have
at it."

"But the parts—"

"You use whatever you need from the junkyard. If it's from inside, just keep an inventory of what you take, and I'll let you have it at cost, okay? If something's unavailable or not in stock, let me know, and either me or T-Bone will help you find it."

If he'd tried to gift the entire thing for free, I would have refused him, but Taylor uttered the magical words. "At cost" was better than fair since he received deep, wholesale discounts.

"Probably going to be the case with an old classic like that."

"Yeah, but I know almost every junkyard from here to Dallas. You need something, holla at me, and I'll get it."

~

My days went on as normal. I returned to full time at the garage, spent a few hours each day after work on my car, then went home and helped my mama around the house. Each day Julia called after dinner to ask me the same series of questions about my arm: whether I noticed any discomfort, rating my pain, if I'd broken anything, and a few other seemingly random inquiries. Sometimes my answers changed, but for the most part, everything was the same.

When the next weekend rolled around, she showed up at the house right as I was finishing mowing the yard and flagged me down.

"Ready to go test your arm?"

"Been testing it, haven't I?"

Her smile widened, but I didn't miss the way her eyes danced over my shirtless chest. "I mean for a shift."

"Yeah?"

"Unless you have other plans…?"

"Nah. Gimme a few minutes to get this all put away."

A quick rinse washed off the sweat, and then I tore ass outside, excited at the prospect of seeing if the arm worked during a shift. I still didn't understand the science behind it, but I understood what it meant. I had already tied my shoes with two hands and signed my name with my left.

Changing to my hound form was different though. No more hobbling or stumbling over my own paws if I went too fast. Last month, I'd gotten amped up while chasing a rabbit and ended up eating dirt.

"So, what do the kids think of your arm?"

"Heh. They think I'm Robocop or something."

Her laughter filled the car. "Pretty cool."

"Yeah," I said. "Pretty fucking awesome. That's, uh, their words."

She laughed again, a small victory for me. "You planning on playing ball with them again this weekend?"

"Yeah, tomorrow after church. It's nice, you know? Used to be that I'd wake up hungover at one of the guys' place and we'd spend the day watching movies while smoking and shooting up." I swallowed and focused my gaze out the windshield. "I was a real worthless piece of shit back then."

"We all have a past. What really matters is who you are now and what you do going forward."

A few months ago, I would have called bullshit on her, but recent experience had shown me she was right. While some folk eyed me with distrust, most people had started to accept me. To treat me like a normal person. It felt good to be welcomed with friendly greetings, and even better to know I'd earned it.

"Yeah. Hopefully they'll see there's more to do than chilling with their pals and doing nothing with their lives. Makes me feel good, too. I used to be in their shoes, so I know how easy it is to fall into that pattern."

"You're doing good by them, Lyle. They know that, and they'll remember."

"Hope so."

Five minutes later we pulled up in Ian's empty driveway.

"Come on in, and we'll get you situated," she invited.

"Nah, I think I'd rather stay outside if you don't mind. I mean, I know you're a guest here, but I feel a little weird without Ian's permission."

"He won't mind. Trust me."

I stood my ground, shaking my head, so she relented and led the way around back. Trees bordered the rear and sides of Ian's yard, providing privacy as well as a windbreak. He owned about a thousand acres of untouched, pristine Texas land, and I'd heard him discussing hunting trips with Taylor and Russ out in the woods. Sometimes that blonde bombshell lioness shifter joined them.

Sasha was her name, and she was the medic who saved my life on the day I lost my arm.

"Are you sure we're okay to be here?" Part of my trepidation was a shifter thing. We didn't like to encroach on someone's territory, but it was also because this was the sheriff's home. As good as he'd been to me, for whatever reason, I still worried he'd never see me as more than the punk he busted years ago.

"Positive. I spoke about it with Ian and Leigh this morning before he left for work."

While I waited in my boxers, Julia ran her fingers over my prosthetic and searched for imperfections or signs of wear. The joints shifted in smooth transitions with a gentle mechanical click barely audible to the human ear. I wouldn't be sneaking up on another shifter any time soon.

"Any tingling or discomfort?"

"Nope."

"And the pain?"

"At the connection site?" I asked.

She nodded.

It was a tolerable ache two days ago, but I felt nothing now. I shook my head and ran my fingers over the rubberlike material designed to provide a safe sheath for my stump. It molded like a second skin, forming a seamless, watertight seal.

"No pain there anymore. That'd be a zero and a smiley face on your scale."

She swatted my chest with the back of her hand, but amusement shined in her eyes. I grinned down at her.

"Per the recent scans, it was a perfect fusion, but I want you to tell me if there's pain at any point during the shift. If it's uncomfortable for your hound, you *must* let me know. Clear?"

"Can I change yet, or did you plan to freeze me to death in this man's backyard?" Of course, that was my fault for being stubborn about not going inside while Ian and Leigh were out. As good as her touch felt, the cold air sort of ruined the enjoyment for me.

When she laughed, a touch of rosy glow touched her cheeks. "Go ahead. I just wanted to check it out before the shift."

The temptation had come over me multiple times in the two weeks since my surgery, but I was finally ready mentally and emotionally as well as physically. I no longer questioned my stroke of good luck and wondered why a bastard like me had received this gift.

"Can't believe how real it is."

"The limb is constructed from a kind of organic metal that we've developed in the laboratory on the cellular level. We call them nanites. The human body doesn't reject them, and anything made from them is light and durable. And it doesn't rust. They were a real breakthrough, but the real test is seeing if they hold up in the field." She began to ramble, talking fast about science and things that flew over my head.

I stared blankly at her.

The same color returned to her face. "Sorry."

"No, no. It's cool. I might not understand what the hell you're talking about, but you're okay to talk about it until you're blue in the face." I mean, if she'd said one more sentence, she probably would have been.

"Feel free to shift."

"You said you'd run with me," I pointed out.

"I am running with you." With a cheeky grin on her face, she pulled a leash out from her coat pocket.

I scowled.

"I'm only kidding." She laughed and tossed the neon green nylon lead off to the side. "Go ahead. The transformation in the limb is activated by the change in your nervous system and an electrical reaction transmitted by the nerves... Sorry."

"I told you, I like it when you talk science." Julia's tendency to apologize only meant someone in the past had shamed her for showing passion in her work.

Aside from a flash twinge of discomfort below my elbow, shifting didn't feel any different. I lowered to all four paws, three flesh and one metal. The arm had shifted and readjusted like clay before my eyes, semi-fluid for mere seconds before it became a canine limb. They'd even given it pseudo claws, little black slivers of curved metal to emulate the real thing on the end of each toe.

Damn, that's cool.

"Let's take this slow." Julia crouched beside me and

inspected the leg. "Go ahead and walk around the yard some. I'm gonna observe and take some notes, okay?"

She monitored and filmed my progress with her tablet while muttering medical babble I didn't understand. Something about the contact of the metacarpal and how it struck the ground.

"And how does it feel?" she asked. "Pain?"

I shook my head.

"Good."

We headed deeper into the woods on uneven terrain, the dirt beneath my four paws, leaves crunching beneath her shoes. The smells of the forest surrounded us, damp grass and old oak leaves, the smell of pine and juniper.

"Take it slow," she coaxed me.

But I was too full of energy, the enthusiasm humming through my body until I picked up speed and took off at a run.

"Hey wait!" Julia called.

I couldn't. I hadn't run on four legs in years. The artificial limb responded beneath me, obeying every twitch of my muscles and adapting to the twists and turns I took between the trees. I sprinted to the side and turned a sharp corner to loop back around behind Julia.

She stared me down at first, trying to play the stern doctor, but a smile tugged at her lips and amusement sparkled in her dark eyes. I barked, jumped around her legs, and wagged my tail.

"Fine, fine, you can run, but only if we test your

coordination, too." She launched a tennis ball through the air.

I shot off like a bullet behind it, too thrilled to be offended by her choice of testing method. I returned seconds later and dropped the slick toy at her feet.

By the time I was ready to take a break, the sun had moved higher in the sky. I collapsed on the deck and stretched out, then rolled onto my back and put on my best begging look. No one could resist a dog belly, not even my stubborn doc. She laughed, relented, and gave me a rub.

"Everything looks good," she said while looking down at the tablet in her lap. Her fingers kept up their work, scratching up and down my chest. "Given a little time, the shift on the limb should come faster, but I think we can call this a success." Then she was gone, pushing up to her feet, all professional again.

I groaned and flopped my head down on my paws.

"C'mon inside to shift," she coaxed me. "Leigh should be home now."

Overcoming my inhibitions about entering Ian's house, I trotted inside behind her.

Leigh popped around the corner with a dishrag in her hands and beamed a big welcoming smile. "Oh, hey, guys. We saw you coming through the window. Hungry?"

"Is it okay if Lyle uses your bathroom to change?"

"Of course. I keep a basket of clothes around for the guys, too, if he wants a shower and a change."

"Doggy!" A curly-haired child streaked across the

floor and wrapped her arms around my neck, practically strangling me. "Mommy, friend for Petunia! Can keep him?"

"Um." Leigh swept in to get her child, but not before I could tickle her with my whiskers.

"He ticklin' me!" With a peal of laughter, she dashed away and evaded her mother.

I spun and pursued the little girl as she wiggled behind Julia's thigh.

"Puppy chase me!" She squealed again with laughter as I caught her; Jules was a sad example of a shield.

"Hey, hey. If you're going to play, do it in the playroom," Leigh chided us. "I'm almost finished making lunch."

Entertaining a kid was the least I could do for Ian and Leigh after all the kindness they'd shown me. Grinning, I let Sophia lead me to the playroom where she threw toys and I ran to fetch them. Eventually, we graduated to a round of hide and seek. I pretended I couldn't find her multiple times. When Sophia was finally tuckered out, I slipped away to shift back. And because I couldn't tell if Leigh's comment about the shower was a polite hint, I used the facilities and emerged without the scent of dog clinging to me.

"I hope you like chicken nuggets and tater tots," Leigh said from the kitchen.

"Sounds great. Where's Julia?"

"She said she had some things to take care of," Leigh replied, "so I told her to go ahead and that I'd give you a lift back to town."

"I'll walk."

She gave me a sympathetic look. A touch of a hand to my shoulder. "Sit down and eat lunch with me. How's the arm working out?"

"It's good," I murmured.

Leigh served me with a plate of crispy nuggets and tots then placed the ketchup bottle within my reach. "Why do you seem so down, then?"

"I'm not down," I said. "Just, uh, thinking about the holidays and all. Presents and stuff for friends and family."

"Anyone in particular? Maybe a certain doctor…?"

Like her husband, Leigh was too observant, and lying wasn't worth the effort. I gave in and nodded.

"I want to get her a gift for Christmas," I admitted between bites. "Has she mentioned anything she'd like? Any interests?"

"You don't know her interests?"

"Science and hiking. She sculpts, too. She told me she makes pottery. Bowls and stuff she gives away to her friends."

"Have you seen her work?"

I shook my head. "No, but I bet she's amazing at it, Leigh. Look at this arm she made me. She's more than a doctor—she's an artist."

And she had every ounce of my respect. I wanted to give back to her for Christmas but heck if I knew what the hell I should buy her. With it just around the corner, I had little time to save. Maybe Taylor would let me do some overtime.

Leigh gestured to the fruit bowl in the middle of the table, its glossy surface gleaming in shades of blue and green with a pattern of waves and cut-out circles around the rim. They varied from as wide as the head of a pin to the size of a pencil eraser tip. "This is one of her pieces. If I were you, I'd shop around online for special glazes. Ian said she's into collecting new colors."

"I wouldn't even know what to look for. Or what she has."

"You coming for Thanksgiving?" she asked.

I blinked. "Uh, yeah? Taylor already laid out the invitation and said it's okay with you guys." I paused. "It is, right?"

"Absolutely. I tell you what. After dinner, when everyone is zoned out watching football or taking naps, I'll help you do some web searching."

"Thanks. I really appreciate that, Leigh."

She smiled and put her hand over mine. "You're not the only one who got a second chance in life, Lyle. I still remember what it was like."

Looking at Leigh now, it was easy to forget she'd had a baby with a joker boyfriend who had ended up in jail, and an addiction to pain medications. She'd turned everything in her life around, and she'd started it on her own, before she met Ian.

"You're a good person, Leigh. I always thought so. Guess that's why I never chased after you."

"God, I can't believe all those years we went to school, I didn't realize you could become a dog."

I grimaced. "After the way I treated you back then, I

don't blame you for blowing me off. Hey...I'm sorry about all that shit."

"Water under the bridge. Thanks for being gentle with Sophia. I've been trying to teach her not to run up to every animal she sees, but—"

I waved it off with my metal hand. "No need to thank me for that. Kids are great. They don't judge and they're always happy to see me."

After lunch I helped clean up before heading out. Leigh tried to convince me to wait for Ian so she could give me a lift, but I told her the truth—I *liked* walking. The weather outside was perfect for a lengthy stroll, and I needed the time to think.

Think about what I planned to do. Julia had mentioned returning to the east coast after the holidays. I had at least that long to prove to her that she meant the world to me.

15

JULIA

*B*usiness back in D.C. had ruined my Thanksgiving plans with everyone, but some things couldn't be handled over the phone.

Our investors, as well as the military leaders authorizing my budget and expenses, wanted to hear the facts about my progress with Lyle. I put together a presentation, answered questions, and took a quiet sense of pride in everything I'd accomplished. The program was a success, and they were all willing to authorize its future and an increased budget.

At the end of the day, I celebrated with a sad turkey dinner from Boston Market and a pint of rum raisin ice cream.

Why did I want to hear his voice so badly and to wish him a Happy Thanksgiving? I phoned Ian's house under the guise of asking if they'd saved me leftovers.

Ian chuckled. "Of course we did. So how'd it go?"

"Ohh, so the all-knowing colonel doesn't know everything, does he?"

"Too distracted with this delicious pumpkin pie to check in on government decision-making, sweetheart."

"Jackass."

"You wanna talk to anyone in particular?"

Yes. "No," I lied. "Just wanted to check in and let you know I'd be back and ready to raid your fridge tomorrow. Take-out sucks."

"Nothing beats Leigh and Dani's cooking. We'll save you a wing or something. Maybe a couple giblets if I'm feeling generous."

A morning flight out of Dulles International returned me to Houston before lunch. I picked up my borrowed car from the garage and made the drive to Quickdraw.

Despite his horrible teasing, Ian presented me with a loaded plate of turkey breast with all the trimmings. "There's more dark meat in the fridge, but I hid this before Lyle and Taylor could find it."

"Thanks. It all smells amazing." Waiting for it to warm up in the microwave was an exercise in patience.

"By the way, I think someone was a little let down that you weren't here."

"Someone," I repeated.

"Uh-huh. Someone who didn't know you'd left town. He even dressed nice for you. Like he was going to church."

"I'm sure it wasn't for me," I mumbled.

"Look, I know you don't want me prying or meddling, but—"

"Then don't."

"But," he continued, "you need to sort this all out. One way or the other. Just sayin'."

Glaring at him over my forkful of mashed potatoes didn't help, because he was right. As usual.

I wanted what Russ, Ian, and Taylor enjoyed with their wives, but of course, the guys had happiness because they pursued what they wanted and didn't wait for the pieces to fall into place. They didn't shove their women away.

"I'm going to drive into town."

Ian grinned and swiped my half-empty plate from my hands. "Go on, then. I'll just finish this up for you."

"Don't you *dare*. You put my damned leftovers back into that fridge where they belong, or so help me I will put your feathered behind in the oven when I get back."

With his appetite, he should have been a buzzard shifter instead of an eagle. I shook my head, grabbed my purse, and headed out. The short drive into town didn't give me much time to think, let alone figure out a plan. I pulled up in front of the garage, turned off the engine, and sat for a minute while my mind buzzed with questions. What would I even say? What if what *I* wanted and what *he* wanted were two completely different things? Sex and affection didn't equal love.

For a logical woman who usually created an organized plan, I had nothing. Which told me to go with my gut and feel out the situation.

Cool wind rustled my hair as I hopped out of the car. I breathed in the refreshing scent of unpolluted Texas air, but I missed the snowfall that sometimes dusted the Baltimore area with a fine layer of ivory in November. It didn't feel like the holidays without it, but Russ said the town would become a Christmas spectacle within the week as decorations flew into every window and the town lit their two intersections with wreaths and colorful lights.

Hands tucked in my pockets, I headed into the garage where Taylor was alone, putting up twinkling lights around the front doorway and windows.

"Hey, Julia. If you're looking for Lyle, he's out back."

Was I that obvious? Mumbling a quick thanks, I headed through, chuckling quietly to myself at the undecorated pine tree by the front desk. Leave it to Taylor to bring on the holiday spirit within a day of gorging himself on turkey and giblets.

Even the junkyard had a Christmas style of its own with multicolored lights glittering from some of the dusty vehicles. I passed an old Chevy decorated with tinsel and turned the corner to find Lyle beneath an ugly green Charger speckled with rust, only his boots sticking out.

"We don't have an appointment today, right?" he called from beneath the vehicle, as if he'd smelled me coming.

He probably had.

"No. No appointment. I thought…" I wasn't even sure. All I knew was I couldn't get him out of my head.

Couldn't get our night off my mind either. And it made me restless. "I wanted to go for a run after dark, and I remembered I'd promised you—in our canine forms," I blurted. "Interested?"

He'd taken the rejection in stride in the month since our night together, but the longing looks didn't end, and like Ian had said, he wore his affections on his sleeve.

"A run?" The work beneath the car ceased, and the area quieted. "Not afraid I'm gonna abuse your trust?"

The words hit like a slap, making me stiffen and my cheeks warm. So much for taking it in stride. "I'll let you get back to work."

As I turned and started to move away, he cursed and a tool thump to the ground.

"Jules, wait, that was shitty of me to say."

I stopped halfway to the door and turned back, spine still rigid. "It's fine. I didn't mean to bother you."

He slid from beneath the car and approached, his boots noisy over the crunchy grass and gravel. "I'm sorry, okay? How's nine for you?"

"Sure." After letting out my pent-up breath, I eyed him warily. "Nine's fine. Want me to meet you here? We can drive out to Ian's property if you'd like. Or do you know someplace better maybe?" Somewhere without a nosy eagle and bear in the area.

He shook his head. "I only have one neighbor out by where I live, and they're across the road. Everything around and behind us is open space, so I use it to run when I'm in the mood." He raised a brow, and the corner of his mouth quirked up in a half smile. "Unless you were wanting to run through his creek."

"No. Definitely not. So I'll meet you up by your house then in a few hours." I lingered though, not quite ready to leave, and looked past him to the car he'd been working on. "Everything going okay with the hand?"

"Yeah. I mean, it's a work in progress, but I haven't wrecked too much aside from stripping a few bolts and causing myself extra work here and there." He shrugged and fell back a few steps to his car to collect the tools arranged over the ground beside it. "See you soon."

Without copping hurt feelings over his polite dismissal, I hurried past Taylor and out to my borrowed car.

"Bye to you too!" he called from the ladder where he strung up the jolly lights. "In a rush?"

"Catch you later, Tay." I didn't want to sit and talk right now; I wanted to smack myself in the head for my stupidity. A run was a great idea, but with Lyle? I was asking for trouble. Stupid, impulsive me.

I wanted to mend things, but I didn't know how. Not really. With a sigh, I pulled away from the curb and returned to Ian's house to hang out with Leigh and Sophia. Ian had gone in to pull night duty at the sheriff's station.

Us girls watched a Disney movie on the couch, and I tried not to fidget as the hours crawled by. At nine, I parked out front of Lyle's, eyed the black windows, and then hiked out behind his house to look for a spot to ditch my clothes. Thankfully his neighbors were far away, and it was pitch black without any streetlamps or house lights on.

The scent of chickens and cats lingered in the area since his mother owned a handful of each for fresh eggs and as snake hunters to keep the pests at bay. In nothing but my skin, I folded a neat pile of clothing as the screen door creaked open and shut at the front of the house. Quickly, I transformed to my coyote body.

"Jules?"

I didn't see him in the dark until he rounded the corner barefoot in only his boxers.

"That you?"

A small yip was the only reply I could give him. I darted out from behind the bushes where I'd changed and playfully leapt between his legs. Rounding back, I nudged his knee with my nose and then sat back on my haunches. Waiting.

"Thought I heard you out here." He crouched down and caressed my face, his touch warm against my fur. I leaned into it and encouraged him to rub behind my ears. Contact between us brought me pleasure I hadn't expected, a deep sense of belonging, as if no man's touch but his belonged on my body. I wriggled in closer and skimmed my nose against his cheek, letting whiskers tickle his scruffy jaw. He laughed.

"Well, ain't you in a good mood? Was that a kiss on the cheek?"

Maybe. Though if I were human, he would have had

more than a kiss to his cheek. I trembled with excitement and nipped his fingers.

"Okay, okay. Gimme a second."

Lyle straightened and hooked a thumb into the elastic band of his boxers to push them down his legs. I tried not to look as they descended the corded, thick muscle of his thighs but couldn't help the magnetic draw between my eyes and his perfect male form. I admired the lean line of his body, his broad shoulders, and the defined chest cut with muscle. Within seconds, I decided it all belonged to me. Only me.

"Like what you see?"

God, yes, and I didn't even have the excuse of being in heat. My gaze traveled to his hips, then I swung around to face the thick copse of trees behind his yard. Chuckling at my reaction, he transformed and lowered to all four paws. He padded up beside me and touched his warm, dry nose against my ear.

I gave in to my impulses, sniffing at his face and neck then rubbing my furred cheek against his before I took off running across the yard toward the nearby trees. It wasn't as forested as Ian's vast property, but we'd have more than enough cover and less chance of encountering wild, local predators.

Then I smelled rabbit on the wind and bolted first.

He caught the scent a split second later and darted after me, hot on my tail. I'd watched him run a few times prior to the surgery, and he'd been fast even with a missing limb. With it back and a week of practice, he was quicker. He looped around a tree in pursuit of our prey, his claws tearing at the damp soil beneath fallen leaves. Autumn air pervaded my senses, the night cool and fragrant.

I lost track of how long we ran, chasing rabbits and squirrels, pinning them down but never killing them. We chased a raccoon up a tree, scared off a fox, and Lyle never slowed once. My excitement was high, the brisk air invigorating and the run pumping me full of adrenaline.

The handsome dog beside me dominated my thoughts, and when we reached a small clearing, I circled around him, rubbing up close, nipping at his heels and scruff. Then I shifted back to my human shape and stood before him as a woman without shame, hoping I hadn't royally screwed things over.

Turmoil coiled in my gut when he didn't join me in his human body. He remained on four legs, gazing up at me with the moon reflected in his brown eyes. My skin prickled with goosebumps, the chilled breeze tightening my nipples into hard points. He let my heart pound inside my chest a moment longer before shifting back and rising to his feet.

"Doesn't hurt when I run now. Not that it hurt much before. Only an occasional twinge and a little pins and needles feeling in my paw."

"You should have told me," I whispered.

"I didn't want to worry you about nothing." He flexed his hand. "You made this perfect, Julia. I kept waiting for shit to go wrong, but it's perfect."

His gaze remained above shoulder level, unflinching from our eye contact.

"That's good." I didn't probe further. Didn't ask him the endless medical questions I could have recalled. None of that mattered right now. Instead, I stepped forward, stopping with only an inch or two of space between our bodies, and looked him straight in the eye. "It wasn't meaningless to me, Lyle. I still feel like I had an unfair advantage, I suppose, but that's not what drove me. I wanted you, plain and simple. I still do."

"Anybody could say the same thing about me, sweetheart. I've done a lot of crap things in my life, but taking advantage of women ain't one of them. Not when they're drunk or drugged up, but I had to have you. And yeah, it worried me that you only did it because you were in heat."

"Heh." I chuckled and shook my head. "Trust me, if I'd wanted to turn you away, I would have. Could have, too. It wasn't the first time a guy's come in at the wrong time, just the first time it was a guy I wanted in return. Still want." My fingers settled at his hips, tracing the indented lines between muscle and bone back and forth in light strokes.

"I'd wanted you since the first day you treated me like a man instead of an ex-junkie. I don't…feel like I'm good enough for you though. I want to be." He moved closer, the stiff part of him brushing against my lower stomach.

"That's what matters. That you want to be. That you're trying to be. You're not the same man anymore,

Lyle. That guy from the past who screwed up? He's gone. People are starting to see that."

The tension melted from his shoulders, and he was practically pliable putty in my hands, giving a content sigh as his fingers wandered down my spine. "You deserve better than me. I'm still trying to put my life together, and you're a doctor, Jules. You fix people and give them new lives again. I'm just a country redneck."

"I'm starting to think I like the country a lot more than the city." Without animal hormones fueling my thoughts, I turned around in his loose embrace, put my back to his chest, and slid up and down his body in a slow, teasing movement until I had his shaft nestled between my cheeks.

He groaned, a low sound that made my inner walls clench with unresolved need. "Dammit, Jules."

My breath quickened as the blunt crown of him glided between my folds.

But he hesitated and withdrew his hips instead of sliding where I wanted him. "Maybe you had it right. Maybe... Fuck, I don't want to say no."

Despite his trepidation, his hands were all over me at once, cool metal and warm skin, the sandpaper texture of calloused fingertips crawling over my right breast and teasing the stiffened peak. I squirmed against him.

"Then don't."

"You tell me something first."

Either he was torturing me on purpose or he was serious about not going ahead with this, which meant

I'd missed my chance. I growled in frustration and wriggled against him, hot and wet, ready for him. I'd been ready since he came out of his house. No, that was a lie. I'd been ready since I asked him out on this run.

"What? What do you want to know?"

"Why don't you have a mate? What were you waiting for?"

The same hand cupped my belly then traced low, and I sucked in a breath, anticipating his fingers between my thighs. He curled his index inward and rubbed my clit in slow circles. I melted against him. This time I was the putty in *his* hands.

"I could ask you the same. I suppose it boils down to never finding someone who sparked my interest. No one who held my attention longer than my work did."

"Prison." A soft chuckle disturbed my hair and sent warm breath against my ear. "Before that, drugs." His fingers moved against me, tracing my slit to gather moisture. He played me expertly, denying me what I wanted and teasing with strong, agile fingers instead.

"Lyle, please."

"I don't have a condom out here. Nothing about our recent relationship led me to think I was gonna get laid."

"I told you I have an IUD," I moaned, writhing in place, grinding against him, doing everything I could to coax him into putting it in me where it belonged.

"Why me?" he asked.

"You said tell me something. Not some *things*," I said in exasperation. One hand lowered to the one he had between my legs, nudging his finger to the precise spot I favored. With my other, I guided the metal limb from my belly back up to my breast. My nipple puckered beneath the cool touch. "Your kindness. Your loyalty. Your dedication. The way you stood up for yourself, even when I was a judgmental bitch." I chuckled, remembering our first meeting.

It had taken him a few weeks, but the time spent working on Taylor's old clunker had been as good as the therapeutic exercises I prescribed for him. He didn't bruise me, though power hummed beneath the metal, and I knew the limits of his strength. One harmless caress after the next teased the stiff peak and clenched my core around the finger gliding between my folds. I moaned and rolled my hips, eager for anything he would give.

"Every day I'm with you, I want you more, Jules. You're more to me than my doctor."

"Right now, I'm not a doctor," I whispered. "I'm a woman who wants your touch. Wants to have you inside of me, deep where you belong. I want...
I want..."

My breath hitched under his next circling press over my clit, my body tensed and tight, ready to snap. He knew it, too, and slowed down, unwilling to grant me my release.

"You want what?" he asked against my ear. His teeth skimmed the curved edge, and then his lips closed around the lobe.

"Claim me!" The plea bust from me, but I'd never

said anything truer in my whole life. "I want you to claim me, Lyle."

He stiffened behind me. His fingers stilled, and he made a long, low groan. "Can't take it back once it's done."

I shivered. Through better or for worse, we'd be tied together for the rest of our lives through the spiritual bond of shifter magic. Years ago, I would have feared the powerful connection between us, would have doubted him and shied away, afraid of what tomorrow might bring. Possible relapse or a return to crime. But I was tired of living my life in fear.

"I think I love you, Jules. And it scares me. God knows I want to keep you as mine, but what if..."

Screw the what-ifs. I could do worse than a man brave enough to fight a gator with his teeth and claws alongside my friends. Worse than a man who had spent every second of the past five months proving he could overcome his past.

"Then claim the woman who loves you right back, and make her yours. I'm not afraid. Not with you." I stepped from his embrace only so I could turn toward him and lower to my knees. I heard his breath hitch when my lips skimmed across his erection.

His eyes glazed over, and his belly tensed. "Jules, what are you doing?"

My fingers crawled over the flat planes and subtle indents defining his abs then glanced up at him. "Making my claim on you because you're mine, and I'll be damned if anyone ever touches it again."

With nothing more to be said between us, I curled my fingers around him, thumb and forefinger nowhere close to touching. Swirling my tongue around his ridged crown earned the sweet reward of a low, guttural groan, one I dedicated all my effort to recreate.

Lyle's thickness stretched my lips around his generous girth. So I held him with one fist at the base once my tongue had the sinewy length gleaming and wet with spit. He groaned again, and his legs trembled as I worked my way from the root of him to the tip. Then his strong hand burrowed into my hair, anchoring me in place.

Mine. Every inch of him was mine.

"Baby." He gasped, "Baby, I'm gonna come."

Our eyes met, and all I saw was raw lust and wild, reckless abandon.

I thrust my head forward, gliding him deeper and letting my tongue massage the veined underbelly. Within moments, I reduced my lover to primitive, animalistic noises, his hips moving and weakened knees almost pitching him down to the grass.

Then I stopped and held him on the threshold until he swore.

"What are you doing?" he demanded, breathless.

I slipped him out of my mouth. "When you come, I want it to be inside me. I want to feel every inch of you, every pulse."

A low growl rumbled in his chest, and it was the sexiest thing I'd heard in my entire life. After releasing my hair, he dropped to his knees before me, leaning forward and claiming my mouth with a hungry, crushing kiss. He urged me toward the grass, but I had another thought in mind. A burning desire I wanted to have fulfilled.

I pulled away first and turned, presenting my back and bottom to him, knees spread and hands planted against the leaf-strewn ground and moist soil. I breathed in the natural musk of our pheromones and quivered with desire.

"Fuck, you're beautiful." His hands molded to the rounded curve of my ass, squeezing and kneading the skin. He took up a position behind me, and I trembled as he entered.

Inch by inch, he filled my warm embrace, forcing my walls to yield to his greater size. The moment he filled me to completion, my composure shattered like glass, and the first orgasm ripped through my body in a series of rhythmic contractions.

"I love the way you respond to me. I haven't even started yet."

He took me by the hips, dragged himself free, then plunged into me anew to bury to the hilt. Pressed inside me balls deep, he whispered, "I love you so much."

"I love you," I breathed in return.

"Love everything about you, sweetheart. You're so damned good to me." He thrust again, churning through my climax and the resistance of my trembling walls, prolonging and enhancing it until I didn't know if the pleasure would ever stop. In the privacy of the woods, we surrendered to lust, uninhibited and unafraid to cry out.

"Say it again, Jules. I want to hear you say it."

"I love you!"

He rewarded my response with a hard thrust that rocked my body forward. My hands slipped on the leaves, and I dropped down to my elbows. The slap of our bodies increased in tempo, faster and faster as we both lost ourselves to the moment. I cried out his name, offered it like a prayer, and begged him to give me more.

When Lyle tensed behind me, he wrapped my hair around his fist and jerked me up against him to place his lips against my nape. His teeth nipped possessively, as dominating as the hand securing a handful of my hair. I cried out as the fiery brand of our bonding jolted straight down my spine, and my second orgasm sent me coasting along on a crazy storm of sensation.

Each time I thought it would end, it began anew in an intense loop of ecstasy and bliss.

He filled me, a hot burst accompanied by a triumphant groan. We rocked as one until we were both too limp to stay up and collapsed against the leaves. His arms wrapped around me.

Everywhere we made contact became hypersensitive, almost too much to bear even a ghostly skim of his fingers. One shift of his hips undid me, and I contracted anew. He nuzzled his cheek against the back of my neck and made a content whimper of noise while stroking my hip with his metal hand.

"My Jules."

I'd stay under the night sky with him until morning if I could. "Your Jules," I agreed, content to remain exactly where we were. Reaching between my thighs, I fondled his balls and the slick connection between us. "My Lyle."

He growled in approval.

I hugged his arms against my chest and closed my eyes, focusing on each breath in and out while my body settled. Every nuzzle and warm breath across my ear stirred my libido, until we eventually went for a slow and languid round two.

Afterward, as our sweat-sheened bodies lay cooling beneath the stars, I smiled and turned my head to catch his lips against mine. "Next time we're doing this in a bed, and I get to be on top."

"I swear you're like an early Christmas gift," he mumbled before kissing my hairline. "Gonna be real pissed if I wake up alone in bed because this is a dream."

"Not a dream, and I'm very happy to be here." I sighed. "Happy is an understatement."

Who would have ever thought this city girl doctor would fall for a country boy?

"Would I sound like a loser if I invite you inside my mom's house?" He palmed one breast and squeezed, brushing his thumb back and forth against the tip. "She's gone tonight. Uh. I kinda gave her a hundred dollars and told her to go have fun with her friend. Said something about eating at Red Lobster and seeing a midnight matinee. She won't be back until tomorrow."

"Did you plan on wooing me?"

"Maybe," he muttered. "Didn't know for sure why you wanted to chill with me."

I chuckled at the thought and rolled over to face him, his semi-soft dick sliding from my body. "No, it's not lame. I'd love to go back to your bed. As long as it wouldn't bother your mom if she found out."

"Ian's helping me find a place of my own to rent, but half the time, I'm not sure if she can make it on her own anymore. Her limp is getting worse." Worry permeated his voice, a sign of a good man who cared about his last living relative. He didn't prey on his mother's kindness; he looked after her. "Baby, as much as she asks me about grandchildren, she'd probably ask you to move in."

Our clothes remained outside, forgotten, as we chased one another into his silent home, the living room lit by only the glow of a television and a pair of Christmas animatronics holding white candles. Before I could get far, Lyle caught me around the waist and hefted me up into his arms, carrying me from the kitchen to his bedroom while we kissed.

I couldn't get enough of him.

"Make love to me, Lyle. All night long."

He lowered me to the bed with a tenderness I hadn't expected, stretching his body over mine without joining us together. He feathered soft kisses from my cheek to my throat, then continued down to my shoulders and collarbone. Each sweet touch sparked against my sensitive skin and dragged me down the path to euphoria. I had never known a lover as thorough as my hound.

"You're the best thing to ever happen to me, Jules, and I plan to show you exactly how much."

16

LYLE

I woke to an empty bed and turned my face into the pillow. Julia's scent was all over it and still fresh, so I figured she hadn't gone far. Still, it took a few minutes for my groggy brain to realize I heard voices from the adjacent room. Feminine voices.

"Shit." I bolted upright in bed, grabbed some jeans from the floor, and hurried into them. Then I shrugged on a T-shirt on my way out of the bedroom door. I found them in the living room, sipping tea before the beat-up coffee table, a shoebox full of old photographs between them.

Mama took Christmas to outlandish levels, decorating every inch of the house in tinsel, garland, and lights. She'd collected these animatronic, ugly angels over the years, and some held candles lit by tiny, flame-shaped 13-watt bulbs while others sang music. The one beside Julia slowly turned to the left and right, waving its phony candle.

"And this is his fifth birthday. No, wait, that's the sixth."

Julia grinned down at the picture my mama held out and laughed. "His Superman jammies are adorable, Mrs. Davis."

"Call me Peggy, baby. Everyone does."

"Mama, you weren't supposed to be back until afternoon," I blurted out.

"Well good morning to you, too, sleepyhead. I know you sometimes have trouble in the mornings with the pain, so we came on back to Quickdraw after our show." She beamed up at me. "I'm so glad I did."

I groaned and fell onto the empty spot beside Julia. "Not the Christmas photos, too."

I hoped Julia didn't catch the comment about my difficult mornings. Lately, I was having strange, phantom aches, and part of me was afraid I'd lose my new arm. Maybe it was childish not to tell her, but I wanted to rule out that it was part of the recovery first.

Julia beamed at me, but I saw the underlying concern in her gaze. "We looked at those first."

She'd likely interrogate me about the pain as soon as my mother was out of earshot. I hadn't felt anything this morning, so I was probably right about it being part of the adjustment.

"I invited Julia to stay for dinner and help decorate the tree."

I groaned. "The tree?" I hadn't dragged it from the shed yet. Even before I was locked up, a couple years had passed since we'd had a real pine tree. I was ashamed to admit I'd blown my mama off more than once about it.

"Yes, the tree, young man. It's been two days since Thanksgiving, so we are a day late."

"I guess I better crawl through fifty years of hoarding to find it, then," I muttered.

Mama pushed up to her feet with her cane and mussed my hair in passing. "You go ahead and do that while I put together some breakfast for both of you."

"I'll help," Julia insisted. She'd thrown on one of my button-down shirts and some flannel pajama bottoms I never wore. They looked better on her.

While they worked in the kitchen, I unearthed even more holiday ornaments, along with a huge cardboard box labeled TREE.

By the time I dragged everything out, my ladies were calling me in to eat before the eggs got cold. I settled at our small kitchenette table and was presented with a plate of meatballs and a bowl of grits.

I eyed them suspiciously. "Those aren't eggs. They're meatballs wrapped in bacon."

"The egg is inside," Mama told me, beaming. "Julia showed me how to make them."

I was too sweaty and starved to argue, and wolfed down two of them before the orange juice was poured. After Julia pressed a cold glass into my hands, I guzzled it down so quickly both women stared.

"Don't push yourself, Lyle," Mama told me.

"I won't. I swear, it's almost like having my own arm back lately."

I spent another two hours outside with the ladder, hanging lights, while Julia alternated between bringing me sweet tea and helping Mama inside.

We never had to explain anything to her. Julia turning up at our house didn't even register as a mild blip on the surprise-o-meter. She shrugged it off, like she'd expected it all along.

Hell, maybe she had. The woman had birthed me after all, and there had never been a damned thing I could hide from her over the years.

At the end of the day, Jules stayed, and while we didn't go at one another with my mother in the house, I held her in my arms the whole night, and wondered how I'd gotten so damn lucky.

17

JULIA

*U*nder normal circumstances, I would have performed the usual trials, recorded my results with Lyle, and gone home. We'd keep tabs on his progress with the arm, and I'd fly in to collect data at scheduled intervals or arrange for him to come to our lab. Now I had all kinds of doubts about home and where it should be.

Texas felt like home, and not only because of my newfound love with Lyle, but the friends I'd missed over the years. Unfortunately, I'd built my entire life around a laboratory in Washington D.C., an ex-fiancé in the Pentagon, and my brother's family in Baltimore. But Lucy and I weren't close friends, and she used *her* family for her support system. She didn't outright deny me visits with my little nephews, but there was always some excuse to avoid a visit or allowing them to stay at my place. She blamed me, and with no love lost between us, we wouldn't be sitting down for Christmas dinner any time soon.

I built the program and designed the prototype replacement limbs, dedicating the past ten years of my life to engineering and medical training. I couldn't walk away from it and turn my life's work over to another doctor.

But I could move my life's work to another location.

As I drove back to Ian's place after being away for a full day, I wasn't surprised to see him on the roof with an inflatable Santa Claus.

"Need any help?" I called up.

"Nah. I got it. So, did you get some?"

"Ian!"

He didn't have to shout it for the entire neighborhood to hear, even though no one lived on the mile-long dirt road except for Russ and Taylor.

"What? Wasn't it only a couple years ago when you told us to treat you like one of the guys?"

"I know for a damned fact you, Taylor, and Russ don't talk to each other that way about your wives."

"Wanna bet?"

I sighed, unwilling to lose money on that one. A smile spread across my face a moment later. "I did get some."

"So why the long face when you got out of the car?"

"Come down and I'll tell you."

He climbed down the ladder, and we took a seat on his porch. The smell of autumn flowers surrounded me, the area filled with pansies and sweet mint in over-sized containers.

"So?"

"We bonded."

"I noticed."

Crap. So much for hoping birds couldn't see or smell those things.

"I love him."

Ian grinned. "I noticed that too. So what's the problem now?"

"My job, Ian. I'm not ready to quit my job. I love my work. Lyle's recovery proves that I have something great, and we can restore complete functionality to our soldiers who lose limbs overseas. How can I walk away from this now?"

"Then don't."

"Lyle can't move to Baltimore with me. This is Peggy's home, and she needs him."

"I'm sure Lyle and Peggy would go wherever you go. She's a sweet woman, ain't she?"

I nodded. "I don't feel right uprooting them like that though, and I guess…I miss you guys, too. Okay? You're like family to me, so it makes sense for me to be the one to move if I can."

"I'm gonna go out on a limb here and assume you've got a plan already, so you're mostly hoping I'm going to make some phone calls and help you make it happen."

Needing his help meant I couldn't wipe the smug look off his face by elbowing him in the kidneys.

I scowled instead. "Maybe. But part of it relies on you being charitable, too."

His brows raised a mile. "*You're* asking for charity? Now I'm intrigued; you never want to accept help from me no matter how sensible the reason."

By the time I finished explaining my ideas to Ian, he was stroking his chin and gazing at the distant fields. "That's not a bad idea."

"Will you help?"

"I'll make the call now. Why don't you go on inside and relax. Sophia's been asking for you anyway. Something about feather braids."

"Good memory on that one." I laughed and stood. "I told her a week ago I'd braid her hair and tie some feathers in like mine."

"Better hop to it. No one holds a grudge like a scorned child."

Sophia rushed to me and crashed into my legs when I entered, so I scooped her into my arms and smothered her small face with kisses. I caught Leigh on the sofa with a book while re-runs of daytime soaps played on the television.

"Oh, hi, Julia. You're only…four or five days late."

"Three," I grumbled. "It's only Sunday."

Leigh and her husband were masters of the smug, self-satisfied look.

With a quiet sigh, I lowered to the couch and set Sophia on the floor. "Bonded," I said to my friend, and then to her child I smiled while gesturing to a tiny, red plastic chair. "Bring that over."

A wide smile spread across Leigh's face. "I figured. How's it feel?"

"Magical."

Sophia hurried away and back with her plastic chair while I pulled a pouch of accessories from my purse. Leigh fetched the brush and water bottle, handing both to me.

"Which colors do you want?" I asked.

"Yellow!"

"Yellow it is."

Leigh chuckled and helped sort some feathers out of the craft bag. She offered the feathers out one by one as I held out a hand for them.

"How about some red, too?"

Sophia scrunched her nose, thought about it hard, then shook her head. "Purple."

By the time I finished, she had half a dozen thin braids woven into her hair, finished with tiny, plastic turquoise beads and an assortment of purple and gold feathers.

"You look beautiful, sweetie," Leigh gushed.

"Who looks beautiful?" Ian asked as he wandered in from his office.

"Daddy!"

Sophia bounced from her chair and launched herself at Ian. He swept her up into his arms and dropped down into his favorite chair where he, bless his heart, took the time to actually indulge her in a girlish discussion. While Sophia wasn't Ian's biological daughter, he treated her as one, a true father to her in every sense of the word.

I envied their happy little family.

I'd wanted my own once, and would have been enjoying blissful, married life if not for what Ian and I dubbed the Fiancé Fiasco. After that, I'd turned all my focus into my work, but with Lyle, that opportunity had possibility again.

"You're looking glowy-eyed," Leigh whispered.

"Huh?"

"Happy. Dreamy," she clarified. "Something on your mind?"

"Oh, ha-ha, no. Just happy to see Ian like this. It's good to see a softer side of him. He likes looking after other people, especially the ones he cares about."

Leigh's eyes misted over with sentimental warmth. "Yeah, it really is," she replied. "And you know what?"

"What?"

"It's good to see the same thing in you. I'm happy you and Lyle found each other."

"Thanks, Leigh. So am I."

"I had a feeling the two of you would hit it off once you got here." Ian grinned over at us once his lap was free. Sophia had run off to her room to play.

I threw a bead at him from the tackle box of hair accessories.

"Fibber."

"What? I did. People have been finding their mates around this little town in droves. It's better than anything you can get at Tinder."

I grimaced, regretting I'd told him about my failed

dating app escapades and the guy who asked if I'd dress up as Pocahontas for him to fulfill his peculiar kinks.

"You're actually serious," I said.

"Dead serious. I found Leigh here, Taylor met Jada, and Dani was renting this same house from me when she met Russ." He stroked his chin. "Plus, I had a hundred dollar bet with Taylor about you two making adorable coydogs. I put my money on you being pregnant by spring when…you know, happens."

"Ian!" He dodged the next bead that I threw at him. Beside me, Leigh chortled.

At least I had confirmation that he didn't realize I'd cycled already, and I'd given his nose too much credit.

"If you throw more stuff at me, I'm not sharing the news I received from General Holcomb."

The threat made me put down the brush I'd been ready to toss. "What'd they say?"

"They'll consider it on two conditions. They're shutting down operations over the holidays, so you have one week to put it together and fly back to D.C. They want to see Lyle in person, and he's got to shift for them to see this arm transform. Videos and photographs won't be enough this time."

My heart leapt in my chest and kicked off at a jackhammer pace. "Agreed."

"Congrats, Jules. You know they'd accept a proposal from you written on scratch paper."

I wouldn't have to sacrifice my career to fulfill my desire to be with my friends again. While blinking away the flurry of tears welling from the corners of my eyes, I rose swiftly from my seat. "I better get working on this."

18

JULIA

*T*hanks to Ian, I had a business plan and a proposal to throw together for the guys in suits with all the pull to make my dreams come true. I planned to expand my operations, and I'd need a considerable amount of money to pull it off.

"Julia, you've been at the computer since the crack of dawn," Leigh said as she moved up behind Ian's computer chair and twirled me around. She pulled me up by both hands and laughed at my startled expression. "It's lunch time. Come out shopping with Sophia and me to get some last-minute Christmas decorations for the big party."

"I really shouldn't. I have to get this fin—"

"A break will be good for your mind. Besides, you've been staring at the same page of your presentation for a half hour. I saw that same photograph of Lyle's arm the last time I passed by."

Heat surged to my face. She was such a lookie-loo, a

good soul with an inquisitive but genuinely caring nature. I couldn't even be mad at her for glancing over the screen when she was right.

"I'm stuck," I admitted. "Usually I'm good at this stuff, but my head is full of cream cheese today."

"Then let's hit the store after a trip to IHOP. We'll put some cream cheese in your tummy then run over to Target. I promise I'll have you back to finish your work a couple hours before Lyle's off at the shop."

In the two weeks since bonding with Lyle, I'd divided my time between sleeping overnight at his place and working during the day in Ian's office. He'd given me free reign of the space while I prepared a presentation that I hoped would sway over the conservative government officials who would have to approve our plan.

Ian and I wanted to open a special rehabilitation center on the outskirts of Quickdraw, and if the military wouldn't fund it, he'd promised to put the money up himself. Fortunately, the years of research belonged to me, and all the necessary patents for my device had been registered in my name. If I left my job, they couldn't take those away.

After applying light makeup to cover my dark circles and braiding Sophia's hair—she wanted Aunt Jewel to do it, not Mommy—I joined Leigh in her SUV, and we drove out for a girls' lunch.

Ravenous after the long morning of sitting hunched over my laptop screen, I ate a massive omelet and

Sophia's bacon, since the little girl had decided she no longer liked pig.

Then I threw up most of it in the restroom.

"I think I ate too fast," I grumbled.

Leigh pushed my ice water into my hand, and I sipped it until we left. Sophia dragged us both up and down the toy aisle in Target but left empty-handed despite her efforts to convince Leigh to purchase a new Lego set.

"Too close to Christmas, kiddo. I'm not buying anything," her mother insisted. Then Leigh subjected us to an hour of her toiling over Christmas stockings and ornaments for the tree.

Stockings. I plucked three from the shelf for Lyle, Peggy, and me.

"Hey, Julia, are you okay?"

"Hm?"

Leigh frowned at me. "You've been rubbing your head for, like, five minutes."

Ian and I called gifted individuals like Leigh "empaths" because of their innate ability to sense and experience the emotions of other people around them. He'd confessed he couldn't even sneak an aching shoulder past his wife without her demanding for him to strip and lie down for a back rub.

"I'm fine. I've just had this headache that won't quit for the past day...or three." More of a migraine than a headache, but I didn't want to bitch and ruin Leigh's holiday spirit with my complaints.

"Have you taken anything for it?"

"A couple of aspirin. I'll be fine, promise."

To prove my point, I dropped my hand from my throbbing temple and forced a smile. Holiday shopping carried on, though I caught my unconvinced friend occasionally glancing at me. Thankfully, Leigh didn't press the issue.

"You guys really go all out for Christmas parties. Don't you have things left over from last year?" I asked.

"Oh yeah. Some of it gets donated, and then some things were ruined because Ian didn't realize all those summer storms put a leak in the roof of the shed." Leigh plucked a bottle of melatonin gummies off the shelf then rounded the pharmacy aisle. She returned with a rectangular, white box in her hand and pressed it into mine. "Um… I think you need one of these," she whispered.

I glanced down at a pregnancy test.

"Oh, sweetie, I don't need this."

Her brows shot up, then she glanced toward Sophia who was playing hopscotch on the floor tiles, oblivious to our discussion. "Aren't you two—"

"Good grief, woman. We *are* but I mean we used protection." I flashed her a weak, uncertain smile, becoming less sure of myself with each word. While it wasn't true for all of us, many female shifters had reproductive cycles to mirror our animal sides.

"I'd feel better if you got it. Just in case, right?"

I bought the test to soothe Leigh's concern, but the truth behind my agreeable gesture was that I needed it to make *me* feel better.

The test would prove one queasy day and a migraine didn't mean I was pregnant.

Once we were back to her place again, I helped her unpackage the holiday goodies and refrigerate the groceries she'd picked up for dinner before returning to the niggling details of my project.

I wondered if Lyle would enjoy our upcoming visit to Baltimore. Over dinner the previous evening, he seemed wary of performing in front of the board, yet eager to help prove my invention was worth the military's continued support.

But first, I needed to finish the presentation packet.

I placed my laptop in hibernate, stuffed it into the bag, and slung the strap on my shoulder before seeking Leigh in the kitchen. "I'm heading to the clinic to finish this all up. Don't hold dinner for me, okay?"

"Drive safe. I'll leave you a plate in the microwave." She beamed. "Unless you go to Lyle and Peggy's."

I'd considered that, but I was half afraid I'd smother him with my anxiety. "Probably not tonight. I think I've exhausted him anyway."

"Trust me, you haven't. I used to think the same about Ian, and he has twenty-five years on your boy."

"Thanks for that *lovely* image," I grumbled.

Leigh's smile widened. "You're welcome."

After hours, the clinic was blissfully quiet and free of distractions. While I appreciated using Ian's office, I also regretted monopolizing it the past few days. That was his man cave, and he had work of his own to do.

I set down a medium coffee I'd fetched along the

way, unpacked my laptop, and slid into the chair. Unfortunately, no amount of silence directed my thoughts where they belonged, and distraction reared its ugly head each time I tried to type the conclusion. My wandering attention span drifted to the blue and white box taunting me from my purse, my mind wondering *what if*.

No. Not possible. Sure, the condom had broken, but I had a device that was 99.9 percent effective. What were the odds?

Then again...

With an irritated huff, I plucked the box up and headed to the bathroom. If this was what it took to get my mind back on work where it belonged, then I'd pee on the stick, tell the negative result 'I told you so,' and move on.

Five minutes later when two pink lines bloomed across the result window, I stared down at the test like a fool.

"How the hell...?"

It had to be a mistake. A dud. I'd probably bought a test with a false positive, but luckily, I knew an accurate way to verify my results.

Taking advantage of the empty clinic, I beelined to the ultrasound machine and plugged it in before wriggling my jeans down my hips and hopping onto the table.

As a woman without children, I'd almost had to move heaven and Earth to get my doctor to agree to place the contraceptive device. He'd wanted to know if my fiancé approved.

A week later, I found a new doctor to perform the procedure. Not that it had been needed since I'd devoted my life afterward to developing the design for a replacement limb, not knowing my own brother would one day need it. Who the hell had time for men and relationships when they were creating breakthroughs in science?

"There's no way…" I muttered while squeezing a dollop of gel on my abdomen. I slid the transducer through the lubrication and placed it an inch above my pubic bone. A grainy black and white image confirmed my theory—the IUD I'd had placed four years ago at the end of a rocky engagement was gone, replaced by an oblong bean with stubby arms. *Two* oblong beans separated by a thin wall. I stared in disbelief at the twin blipping images.

I didn't know the first thing about obstetrics aside from the basics. An appointment would have to be made with my doctor back home in Baltimore while I was in town to present my plan. If someone saw me at the local clinic waiting to see the town's only OB/GYN, word would spread before I had the chance to share it on my own. Gossip traveled fast in a town as small as Quickdraw.

Despite my startling revelation, my heart didn't thrum with panic, and a cool sense of composure fell over me. Peace blanketed my thoughts. As I stared at the blinking, gummy bear shapes in my uterus, I exhaled a pent-up breath and leaned my head back against the crinkling paper on the table.

For years, I'd planned to have children but never found the ideal time in my life. Now, as I embraced a future with a new mate and found success with the greatest invention I'd ever created, I had to wonder about life's plan for me instead.

With tears in my eyes, I thanked the stars and any other primordial force that had a hand in finally giving me what I'd wanted. The career I'd strived to build, fantastic friends, a wonderful man, and two little ones when I'd finally given up all hope. Maybe it *was* possible to have it all.

But would Lyle be happy with the pregnancy? As soon as the doubting, niggling thought flit through my mind, I tried to dismiss it. The voice of reason, her voice ever so small and tiny, barely heard above the pounding of my heart, reminded me of the tender way he'd voluntarily played with Sophia. Was there anyone more right than Lyle, who had already demonstrated his devotion to teens he hadn't even fathered?

About a year ago—two years after having the IUD placed and dumping my ex—I'd considered artificial insemination, desperate to have a child but frustrated with the adoption system. It wasn't as easy as people made it sound, and shifter children were in short supply, preference given to married couples first.

Maybe I wouldn't have picked this moment, this time at the start of our fledgling relationship to conceive, but one glimpse of those little blobby images had sold me on the idea of immediate motherhood.

Now I had to hope Lyle felt the same way.

The next day was when I cried, and it had nothing to do with terror and fear.

I wanted to tell my mother, and she wasn't here to receive the good news. I couldn't phone Daddy to tell him he'd have grandkids to bounce on his knee, because heartbreak had stolen him from me too. And after sharing my joy with Mom and Dad, I would have phoned my twin brother. Too bad depression ripped him away from me too, right?

Death was a cruel mistress.

And while I no longer blamed myself for Charles's death, I mourned him more intensely than ever.

With exception to Lyle, I had no one to tell. No family. No one.

A gentle rap at the door dragged me from my semi-conscious state. I inhaled a deep breath and tasted the air around me, letting the aroma of brewing coffee, frying eggs in butter, and spicy sausage fill my lungs on the next sniff. And Ian. My dearest, oldest friend.

"I'm up, I'm up," I called, barely able to control the sob tightening my throat.

I did have someone. I did have family.

I had Ian. And Leigh. Lovable Russ who tried not to smother me, and sweet Taylor who looked out for me as much as the brother I'd lost. My best friend Sasha who would envy me in secret while providing every ounce of support I needed.

I had the best family anyone could ask for, and no irrational bout of depression would make me forget that. Or swinging, out-of-control hormones for that matter.

"You decent?"

I wiped my cheeks dry with the heel of my palm before I answered. "Yeah."

The door swung open, and Ian stepped inside, dressed for work in his black sheriff's uniform, holstered weapon, cuffs, and radio already worn around his waist. After flashing me a friendly smile, he leaned against the wall beside the doorframe. "I figured you'd be hard at work by now."

A quick glance at the nearby digital clock told me it was half past ten. A couple hours past the time he usually took off in the morning. "Wasn't feeling so good last night."

"Nothing happened between you and Lyle, right?"

"No, we're good."

"Okay. Phew. Russ saw you stayed overnight and had half a mind to go break the boy's legs. It's not that you're unwelcome at our home, mind you, just that we're all accustomed to you and Lyle being joined at the hip when he's not at the job."

"We are *not* joined at the hip, Ian."

"Joined by other places, then."

I scowled and tossed a pillow at him. He batted it

aside and laughed. "Come on. Leigh has breakfast going, and you can practice your speech on me."

After dragging myself to the bathroom to wash my face and brush my teeth, I joined Ian and his family at the kitchen table, praying for a reprieve from the brutal morning sickness of the previous day. I didn't know how I'd take one more day of it, let alone a couple months.

I picked at my eggs and nibbled on buttered toast without an appetite for the slippery, oily egg whites. What was usually a favorite meal turned my stomach and put me off eating altogether until I was only stirring at the food and stalling as much as the child beside me. Watching me closely from the counter, Leigh brought over a steaming mug of tea and a small bowl of oatmeal. This woman made me believe in angels.

And Ian, bless him, remained oblivious.

"You have everything booked for the trip?" he asked as he flipped through the day's paper.

"Yes, Dad. Tickets are bought and a driver arranged for."

He ignored it, accustomed to the teasing he received for his fatherly nature. "How does Lyle feel about the trip?" he asked while maneuvering his coffee beyond Sophia's reach.

The little girl had snuck a mug once and become a nightmare. His words. I only wished I'd been around to witness his plight. The high and mighty Ian MacArthur, taken down by a caffeinated toddler.

"Says he's never been on a plane before, so he's excited and nervous."

"Well, at least he can't hang his head out the window," Ian muttered.

I swatted him. "Go on. Shoo. Go do sheriffy stuff."

"Sheriffy stuff," Sophia parroted. She giggled and shoved her last piece of French toast into her mouth.

Ian rolled his eyes, kissed the top of her head, and then stood. "I'll see you ladies later."

I waved goodbye, Sophia blew him exaggerated smooches, and Leigh met him at the door for a kiss before she returned to collect the dirty dishes from the table and load the washer. I abandoned my seat to help her, but she waved me off.

"You get some rest and relax. If you like the tea I made for you, there's more in the kettle, and it can be re-steeped a couple times."

"Rest?"

Ian had to be right about Leigh's sense of heightened empathy. There were few other reasons for any human to be as intuitive as her.

"You know, that thing you do when you relax and take a break."

I grunted. Living with Leigh and Ian stirred the familiar sense of having a mom and dad again, a blessing and a curse in its own right. He'd chosen his wife well, because Leigh had what I called an "old soul" and a maturity that placed her on our level despite being several years my junior.

"Too much work to do if I want to finish in time, Mother dearest."

Like Ian, she ignored it. "Pace yourself. Don't push yourself. Anyway, Sophia and I are going into Houston for the day to get some clothes shopping done. Need anything while we're out?"

"No, I'm just going to take over Ian's man cave again and try to get the rest of these applications filled out, signed, and scanned. You two have fun and drive safe. Want me to prep up dinner or anything?"

"Oh, no, don't worry about that. Ian's on watch until tomorrow, so he'll grab whatever to eat, and Sophia and I will probably grab something while we're out depending how long this takes."

I gave her a sympathetic smile. Before Charles's accident, I'd gone out shopping with him and his boys. Kids made everything take twice as long.

"Then don't worry about me. I'll eat a sandwich or visit Lyle during his break for lunch at the diner."

Without distractions, I sequestered myself in the office and became lost in the world of board room presentations and government paperwork. Because security was his field of expertise, Ian had assured me it was safe to upload files and that he'd pluck his own feathers if someone hacked him of all people.

If Lyle hadn't called me on my cell around noon, I would have worked straight through lunch.

"Hey. We still gonna meet?"

"Oh! Yes, I'll be right there. I'm sorry."

"It's no problem. See you in a few."

Right. Lunch. I should probably shower first. I channeled my old military days and took a super quick wash down, threw on some clean clothes, and dragged a brush through my hair as I made my way out to the car. Twenty minutes later, I pulled up and spotted Lyle inside at one of the window tables chatting with a pair of old men sipping coffee at the adjacent table.

"Sorry I'm late. I realized I was still in my jammies."

He stood to kiss me. Chastely. He barely brushed his lips over mine, probably because we were surrounded by old people eyeballing our every move. While there had been some initial gossip when we went public, most of Quickdraw's population seemed happy to give Lyle a second chance.

"I could have ordered and brought stuff up to you."

"No, no. I needed to get away from the computer for a bit, so thanks for the call."

"Lasagna is the special today."

My nose wrinkled at the mere thought of garlic, cheese, and meat sauce. "No, I think I'll stick with a sandwich or something."

As my anxiety resurfaced, I wondered for the umpteenth time how and when I should broach the subject of my pregnancy with him. The moment never seemed right, and he had enough worries on his plate. I wanted to get through the meeting first, because everything hinged on the board's decision.

And I needed to see my personal doctor. Needed to know they were okay before we began spreading the news, because the more I considered my lovable hound, the more confident I became about building a family alongside him.

Especially after what he did for Kevin. Within days of Mark Wilson going to jail for domestic violence, the MacArthur family took up a collection plate for Kevin and Hillary. It was enough to get her a small rented house in town.

Lunch arrived within minutes of ordering, a BLT on sourdough for me and chicken tenders and fries for him. At one point, he pushed his plate over and grinned since I'd stolen half of his fries already.

"How much work do you have left?"

"Just the final touches. Proofreading the outline and verifying the figures are correct. Little things that add up to a lot. I promise I'll be done tomorrow."

He tilted his head. "Stayin' over with us tonight, then? You left me in suspense and didn't let me see the last two episodes of that show."

I grinned back at him. "Depends on what time I finish up at Ian's place."

Mourning the distinct lack of Netflix and chilling in the Davis household, I had introduced Lyle to my unlimited data plan, and we'd sprawled in bed watching Marvel superhero shows on my phone instead. Otherwise we relied on their basic cable plan and single television.

I'd have to discover the company serving this area and convince Peggy to let me pay for the works, a satellite with premium channels and all on-demand services.

"You're holding my superheroes hostage from me on purpose."

"I swear I'm not. By the time I shut down last night, I didn't want to do anything but crash."

Skepticism raised his brows, but he didn't call me on my fib. "Well, you're welcome no matter the time. Anyway, I had a talk with Mama before I left for work this morning and figured I may as well give you these. If you want it."

A flick of my gaze to the right determined we had a tiny audience of two, a waitress taking her sweet time at a recently vacated table and the owner wiping down her counter.

He opened his left hand to reveal a small ring with three polished silver, newly cut keys. Each one had a colored rubber band around the top. "This one's to the screen. This one's for the inside door." He tapped his right index finger against each in turn. "This one's the rear door by the kitchen. We don't use it much, and the tumblers stick."

"For me?"

The lopsided smile I adored made its appearance, and his eyes lit up with affection. "Yeah. I know it ain't much right now, but now that I've got a steady job and two working hands, I'm gonna fix it up the way it used to be. Better, hopefully."

Without regard for busybodies and witnesses, I rose from the seat and leaned across the table to take ahold of his coverall's collar and bring him to me for a kiss.

And in one kiss, I tried to convey all my adoration, all my love for him.

"Thank you," I whispered when I let him go.

By the time I had finished the last of his fries, Taylor sent a text asking me to hold on to him a while longer. The guys had a surprise early Christmas gift for him, a difficult to find, rare part for the Charger he was restoring.

I agreed, talked him into a walk through the park, and eventually wandered back with him to witness his awestruck expression when Taylor and T-Bone dragged out a box of miscellaneous parts collected across a dozen junkyards.

It was easy to return to my work after that, inspired by the jovial atmosphere of the shop, our newfound happiness, and Lyle's elated grin. Blending a fruit and veggie smoothie for dinner, I sipped it through a straw, nibbled a few crackers, and backed up my work to an encrypted, external drive.

Leigh and Sophia came back home after dinner hours, peeked in on me, but then they both headed to bed. By the time I finally finished everything I'd set out to do, I spent a few moments debating whether to stay overnight. Peggy would have been in bed hours ago. Lyle, too, as much work as he did, although he didn't keep Ian's old man hours.

But my new keys beckoned.

So I made the drive, helped myself to their home, and tiptoed my way toward his bedroom past the glowing menagerie of robotic Christmas decorations.

After gently shutting the door behind me, I stripped out of my clothes and set them aside.

There wasn't much space in this room for a bed, but at least it wasn't a twin. Most nights when I slept alongside Lyle, we ended up tangled together with our limbs twined, and with their lack of central heating, that was fine with me. A cold draft raised goosebumps on my skin as I crossed the chilly floor to his bedside.

Adorable wasn't the usual way I'd describe my mate, but when Lyle was asleep, no other description would do. The muscles had relaxed in his face, melting away signs of fatigue and stress. He was at peace now. Once I crawled in beside him and beneath the heavy blankets, I ran my fingers through shaggy red hair needing a trim.

Maybe I'd convince him we should visit Jada's spa together.

"Mm… Jules?" His eyes opened, brows drawing close together.

"Sorry. Didn't mean to wake you."

Easing closer and placing one arm around me, he tucked me close against his body. With pajama bottoms and cotton between us, I slid my fingers beneath his shirt to warm them on his chest, then tickled my chilly toes against his ankles, sliding flannel up his shins.

"I thought you weren't comin' tonight."

"Changed my mind."

Snuggling beside Lyle had become my comfort at night, the cramped quarters forgotten once he had his arms around me, breathed me in, his cheek pressed against the hollow of my throat, and his unshaven whiskers abrading my skin.

"Missed you."

"Missed you too."

"Why are you wearing these?" I nudged the waist of his flannel pajamas and pushed them below his hips.

"Because it's forty-five degrees outside tonight." He brushed his lips over mine. "And you weren't here."

"Well, now I am." I tugged his thermal shirt until he shed the layers between us.

Skin against skin, we cuddled close under the heavy blanket, and my fingers trailed over his defined chest, tracing the rise of muscle then the sculpted dips.

"You know, you'll have to get used to how we do winter in Texas."

"There's probably going to be snow in Baltimore when we arrive," I reminded him. "Snow to your shins maybe. If I can survive years of snowy conditions, I can deal with a cool Texas breeze."

He chuckled. "If you say so." Then his face turned against my throat, and he kissed my pulse point. His lips lingered, and a playful nibble almost undid my self-control.

"Lyle," I hissed. "Stop that."

He palmed one breast then rasped his rough thumb pad over the tip. "Stop what?"

As if he didn't know.

"What if we wake your…your…" Groaning out loud and arching my back, I ran my fingers over the back of his head when he took the same nipple between his lips.

He released it with an audible pop. "We won't."

My resolve melted away beneath his kisses and soft caresses.

"How much did you miss me?" The husky warmth of his breath whispered against my ear.

I slid my leg over his hip in invitation. In one stroke, he was mine, joining us in the tight connection I needed, reminding me of how much I couldn't resist his touch. Missing Lyle was about more than missing sex between us.

I'd missed the warmth of his arms. His morning kisses. The way his brown eyes always brimmed with affection. Gazing at my mate, I knew Texas was exactly where I was meant to be.

19

JULIA

$\mathcal{L}$yle tried to convince me to let him purchase his ticket, but after I said I only flew first class and showed him the price, he backed down and relented.

"You didn't lie about the room up here," he muttered while eyeballing the window shutter. "This must have cost a fortune."

I reached across his chest and raised the shutter, knowing what he wanted. "It did, but it's courtesy of the U.S. Government. We have to show them your arm, baby."

"I'm amazed that it didn't go off in the scanner," he muttered.

"I'm not surprised it trigger the machine. We designed it that way."

I hadn't gone through TSA with him, since I had clearance and a Fast Pass to skip the entire production.

I did watch him though, just in case they gave him trouble or it did flag as an anomaly in the search. Lyle had been worried an overzealous agent would glove up for him and he'd have to relive his prison days.

They didn't take him to a private room, but they scanned him a few times, examined it, called a supervisor. He demonstrated it was only a prosthetic and that he was an amputee. It may as well have been flesh since the machines didn't pick up any dangerous materials, the natural polymers a wonderful creation I'd never top again in my lifetime. No, I chastised myself. I *would* top it one day, even if it took another decade or two to figure it out. I'd breathed out a sigh of relief when they finally verified he was harmless and let him through.

Hours later, we landed and I paid for an Uber to ferry us to my house in Washington, D.C.

What the hell was I going to do with it? I'd have to contact a realtor, or at the very least, decide if I wanted the hassle of hiring a property manager to rent it out. Shifters never broke their bonds, and divorce from Lyle wouldn't be a choice.

I believed him when he said he'd changed his ways to become a better man, because I could feel the honesty in his soul and the jubilation he experienced whenever he made the next improvement in his life.

He shouldered his backpack and brought my carryon while I fished out my house key. I lived in a four-bedroom, two story townhouse in the suburbs, and although I didn't need the space, I had loved it at first sight and wanted it to be mine.

Lyle fell back a few steps behind me, staring at the spacious floor plan. Chocolate hardwood floors stretched before us into the living room and kitchen, and a dark staircase led to the second floor.

"Holy shit. You're going to leave this behind to come live with us?"

"Home is with you," I replied.

And our twins, I thought. I didn't know when to share the news with him. Had I been given an option, I would have waited a year or two before bringing up the subject of a child. Given him a chance to attend school and finish sorting out his life. But that wasn't the game fate wanted to play with us.

Though my pregnancy complicated things in our new life, I wouldn't change a thing. I wanted these twins, and I wanted him, and if the board agreed with the plan Ian and I created, no sacrifices had to be made. We could have it all.

"Make yourself comfortable," I told him. "I'll get the heat turned up."

It didn't take long to get situated. I eyed my empty fridge and pathetic pantry selection with a frown, then pulled out a bunch of to-go menus.

"Order in or do you want to go out somewhere?"

Lyle poked his head into the kitchen and looked around. "Are you tired?"

"Not really."

"Then why don't you show me around a little?"

"Fine." I laughed and put the menus away. "There's a

little pizzeria down the street if that sounds okay. The house should be all warmed up by then."

Bundling up for the frosty weather, we headed out arm in arm. The sidewalks had been shoveled clean of snow, making for an easy, hazard-free walk. The neighborhood was quiet, which I'd always liked about it. We passed a few snowmen in yards and lots of twinkling lights, along with the occasional Nativity scene depicting the birth of Christ.

Religious preferences were yet another thing I'd have to discover about my new mate. No matter how much I learned about him, there always seemed to be more I hadn't learned during our whirlwind romance. Church hadn't been a large part of my upbringing, and while it didn't seem to be of incredible importance to Lyle, I also hadn't asked.

I sighed.

Lyle cocked a brow, picking up on my restless thoughts. "What's wrong?"

Had he always been so intuitive, or had it only developed more since our bonding?

"Oh, nothing. I was only thinking about how close we are to Christmas. Do you and your mom do anything special?"

"No, not really. Well, Mama goes to Mass, but I haven't gone since I was a kid. She used to call me a heathen, but she's over it for the most part." He blushed. "That's okay with you, right? I mean, if you wanna go, I'm cool and we can—"

And instantly, I felt better. "Then we'll be heathens together," I whispered before kissing his chilly cheek.

When we reached our destination, he held the door and shooed me inside ahead of him. Warm air smelling of sauce and spices enveloped us as we stepped inside the pizzeria. I peeled off my gloves and shoved them in my coat pocket while a smiling waitress came over and asked if it was just the two of us tonight. Then she led us to a table along the wall where we had a perfect view of the large brick oven, left us with menus, and promised to be right back.

"What sort of toppings are these?" Lyle stared down at the menu. "Figs? Isn't that what's in those gross cookie bars?"

"Artisan pizzas. Look, they have some normalish ones. How about meatball?"

"I… I'll just take your word for it. I mean, I've eaten worse." He rubbed his head behind one ear and squinted at the menu.

We settled on two small pizzas, and while he tried one of the seasonal beers, I asked for water with lemon.

"You really sure about this?" Lyle asked with an impulsive edge to his question.

"About what? About eating pizza?"

"Leaving all this. That's… You have a really nice home, Jules. And places like this with your fancy pizza and beer. Not that this isn't damned good," he said, looking at the bottle again.

"I can get pizza anywhere. Beer, too. What I can't

get anywhere else is you." I reached across the table, took his hand, and squeezed it.

"I don't want you to have any regrets, is all."

"I don't and I won't."

He raised my hand to his lips and kissed my knuckles. "Still can't believe you're mine. There's some days where I think I'll wake up in prison again because this is a messed up dream. Messed up like it's too good to be true."

"Nope. All real, I promise."

The arrival of our food broke us apart. Despite his initial reservations, Lyle took a slice of each to try. His surprised and pleased look after trying the fig and prosciutto with goat cheese made me laugh, but I refused to say I told him so.

I took a slice of each and said a small prayer to any god that was listening that I wouldn't ruin our first and true date night by puking all over the pizzeria bathroom. For all the time we'd officially been together, there had been no time for evenings out, and I'd made a genuine effort to alleviate Lyle of any pressure to spend his hard-earned wages on me.

Money was the last thing I wanted from him. I loved his loyalty and knowing I could depend on him for anything.

"You ready for tomorrow?"

"As ready as I can be." He grinned then scarfed down the last slice of meatball pizza, obliterating any chance we had of taking home leftovers when he dragged the box with my last two servings across the table.

The journey home cleared my head and made my sensitive stomach feel better. I didn't know if it was the crisp air or the walk itself, but I was glad the nausea stopped by the time we got inside. We showered together in my master bath and then crawled into bed. Cozied up against him beneath the blankets, I was snug and warm, ready to face what tomorrow brought us.

20

LYLE

*C*ompared to Quickdraw, any place was a wonder to marvel at and appreciate, but the nation's capital was truly impressive. Julia looked like she belonged here, and the first niggling doubts crept into my mind. How long would it take, I wondered, until she resented me for taking her away from this?

Sure, we were bonded, but that didn't mean shifters didn't develop love/hate relationships with their soulmates. A soulbond didn't wave some magical wand promising a pair would never argue and fight again. It didn't mean there wouldn't be disagreements and all the stuff that afflicted normal, everyday human couples.

It meant for as long as she lived, I'd never love another woman as much as I loved Julia, and the same was true for her. It meant no matter how angry she made me, her well-being would always be my priority.

I could hate her in one breath and simultaneously love her in the next until I was heartsick.

But just the same, I hoped and prayed to God it'd never become like that.

Trusting in her and loving her also meant believing her, and if she said she was ready to leave this shit behind, I had to accept it as my gospel. Julia would be happy in Texas, surrounded by her friends.

"You should see this in the spring when the cherry trees are in bloom," she told me as we walked arm in arm down through the National Mall.

I tried not to shiver. "The snow is pretty."

Every so often we got an inch or two back home, but it always melted off the same day. This was different. Four inches of the white stuff covered the ground in a white blanket. The paths were clear at least, and salt and pea gravel crunched beneath our boots.

It hadn't taken long to decide I didn't like the cold. My nose and cheeks burned.

"We're almost there," she assured me, practically radiant with the joy of being home again.

"Do they know we're...?"

"None of their business. I'm not hiding it, but there's no need to mention it either."

I exhaled a sigh of relief and nodded. "Okay."

A few minutes later, the ominous building loomed before us, and my heart began to pound like a drum. This was the moment that would make or break her entire project, the difference between living in Quickdraw with me and Mama or keeping up a long-distance relationship.

Hell, I'd do it for her. Not that I had a choice, irrevocably bonded to her. Mama and I had discussed it the previous day and decided if Julia didn't receive approval for her ambitious project, she'd sell the house and move in with a friend while I moved to D.C. with my mate.

Julia used her credentials to gain me access at several checkpoints. My palm was slick with sweat by the time we approached the door.

Six people awaited us at a conference table. The smell of coffee and sugary pastries assaulted my nose. I didn't know much about military ranks, but four of the people inside wore an impressive array of gold stripes and shiny stars on their uniforms. The other two wore the same sort of lab coat I'd seen Julia in a hundred times. Doctors.

"Welcome Dr. Bearheart. Mr. Davis," the woman at the head of the table greeted us. She rose and shook Julia's hand, as did the other five while giving me curious looks.

"Admiral Breckinridge, good to see you again," Julia replied. "This is Lyle Davis, and he's grateful to provide this demonstration for the board."

All six sets of eyes turned on me.

"Thanks for having me up here, and for the opportunity."

One by one, the board members introduced themselves by title, name, and their branches, though I'd be lucky to remember a single one. My stomach churned into a tight ball of tension in my gut. What if I fucked something up for her?

As we took our seats, Julia reached for my hand beneath the table and squeezed my fingers in reassurance. Through our bond I found my composure, taking a deep breath to settle my racing heart and churning stomach.

The entire thing began with a digital presentation on the projector. I didn't understand a word of her scientific jargon, but I loved watching the way her face lit up as she talked. Slide after slide she took them through the entire process, from the initial studies up to her first patient. A photograph of a handsome, native man in uniform came up on the screen.

He looked like her. It was in the set of his eyes and nose, and the wide, friendly smile. Her twin.

She paused there for a few minutes to discuss successfully finding a matching recipient—*me*—and the adjustments required to make the limb compatible. After that, she moved on to my case, which included video highlights from the surgery and our first field test in my hound form. Thankfully she left out the ball toss.

"An impressive undertaking," the stern-faced man seated across from me said. General Hallis-something. "Tell me, Mr. Davis, how has this arm helped you? Do you find it gives you back the full range of mobility you lost?"

"I'm a mechanic by trade. Without it, I couldn't

work on cars anymore. My boss had me pushing a broom and ringing up customers at the checkout. I'm also my disabled mother's caretaker, and she's needed my help around the house. I do it, but it's a struggle holding and hammering a nail with only one hand, let me tell you." I went on to detail how I'd adapted to running on three legs, but that it never compared to being whole.

"Thank you. That's quite helpful."

The doctors asked me a load of questions, everything from how it felt, to whether it performed to my expectations.

"Better," I replied. "If there's a delay, I don't notice it."

"And you have no difficulties in controlling the strength of your grip?"

"A little at first, but Doctor Bearheart has that under control. She made adjustments and led me through exercises."

"Excellent. Now, I'm sure we're all in agreement here that we'd like to see the process in action. Could you shift for us please, Mr. Davis?" the admiral requested.

Even knowing they'd ask, I still experienced a stab of uncertainty. Stripping down in front of a room of old ass military officers and doctors was better than disrobing for a hallway of correctional officers eager to see if I had a knife wedged between my cheeks though.

"Uh, yeah. Sure." I shed everything but my boxers and moved to the front of the room.

Would a hound look funny in a pair of shorts? Sure. Still, it beat waving my dick around for them all to see. That was for Julia's eyes only.

The admiral's eyes traveled over my chest, then she cleared her throat and glanced away. I caught one of the generals eyeballing me a little too close for comfort, too, when he thought no one was aware of *where* his attention had fallen.

Murmurs went up as I made the shift, and more than one person stood to peer over the table for a better look.

"Look at that. Quite impressive."

"Hardly any delay in the restructuring."

"The nanites learn," Julia spoke up. "They respond faster each time, making the transition seamless."

Might as well put on a show, I figured. After shaking off the clothes from my hindquarters, I jogged around the table, giving each board member a chance to view the limb in motion.

"And you can reproduce this, Dr. Bearheart?"

"Yes, General Hallister, I can. With the right candidates willing to make the required lifestyle changes and dedicate the time needed for a prosthetic replacement, we can give back our wounded soldiers, as well as our shifters, their mobility. Of course, each one is built to suit the person's needs. There's no mass producing limbs to have on hand. This limb took me over a year to make, and as I refine the process, I estimate at peak efficiency I can create one per three months."

"And with a team?"

"As many as needed."

"Christ. This technology puts us ahead of Russia," one of the military doctors said.

"And China," another general mused, rubbing his chin.

No one seemed to mind or notice that I stayed in my hound shape. I leapt into the chair beside Julia and tried to look dignified.

"Is it truly necessary to move the facility to Texas?" General Hallister asked. He rubbed his chin and frowned down at the tablet in front of him. "It seems extreme to move it out so far from D.C."

"There's no better place to put our shapeshifting soldiers through the rigorous physical therapy I've required of Lyle. Colonel Ian MacArthur has generously donated a large tract of land for the project. It's secluded, and better yet, it's free."

"Saving us the cost of buying land. Clever." Admiral Breckinridge smiled.

Julia inclined her head. "Of course. And, because there are a few shifters living in town, any future patients will gain a support system of relatable people. People who can work with them in a way human doctors alone can't."

"Agreed," Dr. Killian said. "I've only worked with a handful of your people and find myself at a loss."

I glanced around the table at nodding heads and intrigued faces, each one supportive of her idea.

There hadn't been a single word of dissent.

Not one.

"You'll have your facility, Dr. Bearheart, and a team. We'll meet again after the new year to put plans into motion," the admiral said.

One by one, the officers and doctors left after exchanging goodbyes with Julia. One or two wandered toward me but seemed to lose their nerve at the last second, or recall that I was a person and not a dog hanging out for scratches.

When the room emptied at long last, I watched with amusement as my mate did a little victory dance, punching a fist in the air that was at odds with her professional appearance. Caught up in her enthusiasm, I leapt down from the chair and bounced around her legs.

"Did you hear that? We did it. We're going to get our facility!"

Ours. The word made my stomach do a funny little flip and filled me with warmth. Julia dropped down to her knees, took my head between her hands, and kissed the tip of my nose.

"You can leave on two feet or four, but I'm going to warn you, the ice outside is cold, and I can't take you into the museums or anywhere to eat like this." She paused, then grinned before adding, "Or we could hurry home, order in, and not leave the bed until tomorrow."

The wicked sparkle in her eyes left one option. I eagerly loped toward the door.

At least it was only a short trip to the car, right?

21

LYLE

*H*oliday lights twinkling from the eaves and every window greeted us when we arrived at the MacArthur residence, but they were nothing compared to the ten-foot-tall, blow-up snowman on the yard. Frosty waved to us and blasted cheerful holiday tunes.

"You okay?" Julia asked.

"Yeah. I guess I'm not used to this sort of thing, is all."

"What? Parties?"

"The legit kind, yeah." I chuckled and turned in my seat to face her over the center console. "Thanksgiving was the first time I've really been a part of a good group, you know? And I sat by myself most of the time. Ian said they didn't want to crowd me." Though he'd invited me later that evening to go Black Friday shopping with him, Russ, and Taylor, I'd bowed out when the department store floor plans came out. Those guys treated shopping like a covert military operation.

"I'm sorry I wasn't there."

"Nah, baby, it's all good. Just new is all."

She leaned over and nipped my chin, then followed up with a slow and tender kiss that had me itching to drag her over to christen my new ride.

Maybe later.

"We could skip out," she whispered against my lips, reading my mind.

The temptation was real, but at the same time, I'd been looking forward to a real Christmas celebration. "Come on, sexy. We're expected and they already spotted us."

Sophia stood in the open doorway bouncing up and down on her tiny feet. I could hear bells tinkling from here.

"Fine," Julia groaned. "But I'm taking advantage of you later."

I grinned. "Be my guest."

Since our return from D.C. last week, we'd been unable to keep our hands off one another. With no work for her to do beyond a wish list for her facility, and reduced holiday hours at the garage, we had plenty of time to indulge, so we'd stayed a few extra days.

Never did get around to seeing those museums, but we did visit other places and create a list of destinations for the next trip.

We climbed out and headed to the house with gifts

in tow. Gifts I ended up juggling in my arms when Julia passed hers over so she could lift Sophia up.

"Ooof, you're heavy," Julia teased. "Aren't you supposed to be in bed?"

"Santa comes after midnight," the little girl told us in a serious voice.

"Ah. Right. My mistake. I guess that means you can party some first."

A few steps in the door and Leigh came to our rescue. She shooed her daughter off to play and grabbed a part of my armload. "You can put the presents over there under the tree, Lyle. I'm going to steal Julia for a minute to help Dani and me in the kitchen."

Ian's house had been transformed into a veritable Christmas wonderland. Tinsel-bedecked garlands were strung up everywhere I turned, joined by a menagerie of holiday themed animatronic decorations, stuffed bears in Santa hats, and even a train chugging around the base of the tree. Cheery holiday tunes played over the speakers at a low volume, and the whole place smelled like fresh pine.

Sophia played on the floor with Mateo, Russ and Dani's son. They had a pile of wooden blocks between them that the younger boy was building into stacks which he then knocked down. Each time his towers crumbled, he clapped his chubby hands together and laughed.

Watching them made me smile.

"Hey, Lyle, you got a minute?"

Looking up from the kids, I spotted their dads coming in from the back porch.

Russ was a huge guy, his biceps easily as thick as my legs. I swallowed and watched him approach with Ian at his side, expecting them to drag me outside to rough me up in the backyard for an imagined slight. Russ walked with a hard ass stride that could make trees uproot themselves and dive for cover. And he was coming toward *me*.

"Heard you're courtin' Julia," Russ said.

"A little more than courting if they're bonded," Ian pointed out.

Russ grunted. "These youngins are always putting the cart before the horse."

Ian gave him a warning look, and the bear shifter sighed.

"I love her, and I'm not going to fall back to my old ways," I said, standing my ground. "You have my word on that. I'm gonna take good care of her."

"You had better. I want you to know that if you mess up, I have a backhoe and enough land for no one to ever find you."

"Can we not give death threats on Christmas Eve?" Ian cut in.

"I didn't say anything about killing him first."

I cringed.

"Anyway, that's not what we wanted you for. Here. This is a Christmas gift from us."

"I thought we were doing some group gift game thing." That's what Julia had said, at least. We'd each brought one present for the game and pooled money together to buy gifts for the kids.

"Nah, you're good, dude. This is in addition to the game. Consider it a gift from us to you and Mrs. Davis," Taylor chimed in as he joined us.

Russ passed over a slim, plastic tube with a black end cap. I tugged it off, and a rolled sheet of paper bounced out into my hand. "What *is* it?"

"Take a look," he said.

Unrolling the paper over the nearest table revealed a floor plan of Mama's house. Ian held down the far end of the large blueprints while I stared at drawings of an additional three bedrooms, a second full bath, and a screened front porch beside a proper garage and driveway.

"Russ and I drew these up together and had a talk with your mama about whether or not it's fine with her," Ian said. "Truth is, she does need your help. She wants you home, but she doesn't want you to feel like a burden either."

Taylor stepped up to my left side and placed an arm around my shoulders. "And I don't want to lose one of my best employees by letting you move to Huntsville to find work there. You've been with this shop since Tito's days, and believe it or not, there are people who still drive up asking for you to work on their shit, dawg."

I stared at the blueprints and estimated thousands of dollars in labor and materials. "How's this going to happen?"

"We're going to build it for you," Russ said.

"But the cost—"

"Yeah. About that." Ian grinned and waved his wife over.

Smiling, Leigh crossed the room with a red velvet sack and tossed it onto the table. Colorful cards filled the pouch, a treasure trove of Hallmark phrases and handwritten pieces of cardboard with Polaroid photos of my favorite teens.

"All the kids helped out, and the church passed around the donation plate this past Sunday," Leigh explained. "Russ thinks there's more than enough to cover the cost of building supplies."

I tried to swallow, but emotion pressed against my throat and made my windpipe feel as narrow as a pin. "No, I can't accept this. It's too much."

Ian chuckled. "You can and you will. The community wants to help, Lyle. This isn't about just you now. It's for your mother, too."

The overwhelming generosity stunned me and quickly threatened my composure. I blinked a few times, but my pride took hold and managed to hang on strong. No way was I going to cry in front of these guys.

"Dude, y'all are too good to me."

"You got one more gift coming just from me." Taylor reached in his pocket then tossed a keyring to me.

"What's this?" I eyed the key in confusion.

"What's it look like? Welcome to management."

I flipped over the keychain to reveal the cat logo
etched in silver.

"When you finish school in a couple years, I want to
make you a full partner in the garage."

"What about the other guys? Taylor, I've been gone
for years. No one's going to respect me receiving part
ownership of this place—*your* place."

"We talked it over, and even T-Bone agrees this is
the right thing to do. He's heading back to school to get
his kinesiology degree next month anyway, so I need
you to step up and take his place. Nobody wants the
responsibility of being the assistant manager, and you
were here first technically. You work harder and longer
hours than everyone else, especially since I began
letting you under the hood again."

"I don't know what to say."

"Say you'll take it." Taylor's grin widened. "I have
big plans on expanding the business to include motor-
cycles, too. And I'd like to open another shop over in
Huntsville, but I can't do it all myself."

"Yeah, man. I mean, thanks. This…this is great."

I glanced up to notice Julia and Ian coming over
from the stairs, realizing I'd been so distracted with
Taylor's gift I never noticed the eagle leave. Julia held a
pink, cardboard shoebox in her hands, and she had a
big grin on her face when she approached.

"One special gift from me now, baby."

"You didn't have to buy me any…"

A familiar smell reached my nose before she even
removed the lid. Inside the box sat my black cat, a few

months older and a couple pounds fatter than I remembered, with a nylon collar around his neck and a shiny metal tag.

"You found my cat from prison," I breathed.

His yellow eyes raised to my face, then he sprang out of the box into my arms. Taylor crowed with laughter, but I didn't care and ignored his smug face. With every gift, my friends outdid themselves, and it took all my effort not to cry like a big man-child in front of them.

"Jules, how'd you do this? I didn't think I'd ever get him back."

Tux thrust his head beneath my chin and purred, the smell of shampoo still fresh on his fur. Someone must have been feeling brave as hell, but he'd obviously recovered from the ordeal. His whiskers tickled across my cheek, and I held him close. For three years, this cat had been my best friend. He'd gotten me through rough times and even harder times when I'd wanted to give up.

Julia would never know what she'd done for me.

"Ian did the work. All I did was ask him if it was possible to get a cat off prison property."

"Warden Richards didn't mind after I buttered him up a little. One of the inmates on the janitorial crew caught the little stinker and brought him out to the gates for us."

"Jules, you're the best." I pulled her close with one arm and kissed her while our friends hooted and hollered, exaggerating an applause.

The rest of the evening passed by with merriment I hadn't enjoyed in years. The kids ran through the house trying to sneak presents from under the tree until we all caved and let them each open one. After they were tucked into bed upstairs, we adults enjoyed a hilarious game of gift stealing. By the time we finished, I ended up with a Netflix gift card tucked into a popcorn bowl filled with candy bars and other movie-watching goodies for two. Julia stole a mini-keg of craft beer out from Ian, who had stolen it from me after I stole it from Daniela.

She gave me a self-satisfied smile and stuck her tongue out at me when I reached for it, twisting to the side and guarding it from my hands.

"You don't even drink beer," I grumbled.

"No, I don't drink *cheap* beer," she clarified.

We were one of the last couples to leave just before midnight. Jules was our designated driver, because I'd imbibed for once and enjoyed too much eggnog with Russ and Taylor. Tux snuggled in my lap during the drive home, his motorboat purr making us both laugh. He'd been louder than the radio.

As we parked out on the street, I thought back to the plans the guys had drawn up. It was gonna be nice having a driveway. I could put up a basketball hoop. Someplace to play with the boys when they visited. Kevin's life had taken an awesome turn for the better, and I had a big gift under the tree from him and Hillary I'd open in the morning.

"Everything is set up inside for Tux," Julia said while

we unloaded the car. Leigh had sent us home with Tupperware bowls filled with leftovers. "We also had him chipped, since I figure he's used to being outside."

"Damn, you really thought of everything."

"I wanted you to have something that makes you happy."

After I released Tux to explore his new home, I turned and pulled my mate into my arms. I skimmed my nose against her throat and breathed her in. I didn't know what it was, but something about her scent had recently changed, making it more alluring than ever.

"*You* make me happy. But this… Thank you, Jules. I never expected to see him again."

"Come on. Let's go sit outside."

"What, you wanna watch for Santa?"

"Maybe." She grinned up at me. "Or maybe I just wanna watch the stars for a bit with my guy so we don't wake your mama up."

"Good plan. Wanna go to the back?" I raised my eyebrows suggestively. "I'll keep you warm."

Julia rolled her eyes. "I'm not getting in the frigid grass with you tonight, even if it is Christmas Eve."

I grabbed a plate of cookies to bring out with us. The old swing bench on the porch creaked when we sat down. For a while we cuddled in silence, munching on gingerbread men and iced sugar cookie reindeer. After all the hustle and bustle at the party, I welcomed the quiet moment and the chance to hold her close.

"This is like the best day of my life," I muttered. "I still can't believe it. Fixing Mama's house and starting school next month. Partners with Taylor. You found Tux. Fuck, I missed that little asshole. I don't think it gets any bet—"

"I'm pregnant."

My foot pressed against the porch, halting our swing, and I turned my face to stare at her. "What?"

Julia nibbled her lower lip then smiled and repeated the quiet words with more volume. "I'm pregnant. You're going to be a daddy."

I blinked at her. "How'd that happen?"

"Well, when a boy and a girl like each other very much—"

"I know that part," I said. "Baby, you told me you had one of them *things*."

A combination of uncertainty and amusement flit across her face, a wavering smile that threatened to vanish at any moment if I said the wrong thing. But I didn't know what to say. I pulled her closer instead and tried to convey any feelings of reassurance she needed.

"I had one, but apparently it fell out. I don't know when I lost it because nothing changed for me, but that day in my office…"

A kid. I'd never thought about having one of my own. Most of my old friends in high school had a score of baby mamas and all kinds of drama surrounding it. But I'd never been involved, because if there was one thing my mother taught me, it was to wrap my shit up.

"What about your work?"

"What? I can't be pregnant and work at the same time?"

Heat rushed to my face. "No, that's not what I meant—"

She brushed a kiss against my cheek. "I know. And it'll be fine."

"You're...not upset that I got you pregnant?" The news made my blood run hot with excitement and jubilation born from a rush of alpha male pride. I'd made a kid. Hell yeah. But I couldn't show my elation yet, bottling it in until I knew Julia's thoughts on the matter.

"Would I have preferred to plan it? Sure. But am I upset?" Julia shook her head. "I'm thirty-seven years old and not getting any younger. I wish..." Her fingers interlaced with mine. "I wish my brother and my parents were here to see it, but I'll settle for Peggy getting the grandchildren she's wanted."

"She's going to fuss over you so much."

Julia's smile returned. "I can live with that. What about you? Is this... Are you okay with this?"

"You know, I never thought I'd make a good dad since I never had one of my own, but helping out the youth program and seeing Ian and Russ with theirs made me realize I can do better than he did by just being there. So yeah, I'm okay."

"You'll make a great dad. The twins will be lucky to have you."

"Twins?" My eyes widened, and my hand touched her flat belly.

Her smile and eyes brightened. "Twins."

I kissed her, hard and swift, every ounce of my love

for her poured into the gesture. Julia leaned in close, body soft but her kiss equally as hungry. She tasted like sweet and spicy apple cider, and I couldn't get enough of her. My fingers curled in against her tummy, drawing her sweater up so I could sweep my touch against her skin. It was hard to believe two little lives stirred there. Two lives I'd helped create.

Driven by the need for air, our lips parted, but I couldn't bear to move away yet. Julia laughed as I scattered kisses across her nose and cheeks.

"I better not be dreaming this, baby."

Julia pulled back enough to look me in the eye and frame my face between her slender hands. "No dream. I promise."

"Good."

I kissed her again, gentle this time, slow and tender, until she was practically melted into a gooey puddle in my arms. That was another thing I loved about my little coyote, how she went from tough and unbendable to pliant and vulnerable. That she trusted me enough to let down her guard.

Breaking away, I pressed a final kiss to the tip of her nose. "Stay here a second. I'll be right back."

I left her on the swing and hurried back through the house, moving quiet enough not to wake Mama by stumbling over her tightly packed Christmas displays and making a ruckus. It took only moments to find the present I'd hidden away in my room. I returned with Julia's gift in my hand.

"Close your eyes," I called from the doorway before

I stepped outside. My clammy palms itched. For a moment, I wondered if I should sit back down beside her or drop to a knee.

No. If I did any single thing in my life with confidence, it had to be this. I kneeled in front of her, took the ring from its velvet box, and held it up between my thumb and forefinger.

"You can look now."

Julia's eyes opened, and her gaze snapped down to the ring. It wasn't much; the sterling silver with a central fire opal flanked by two turquoise stones had been a little more than two weeks' pay. Blue and red flashes sparked within the opal beneath the twinkling Christmas lights.

"It should fit—I mean, I hope it does. I, uh, borrowed one of yours while you were showering and traced the inside circumference." I turned one of Julia's hands palm up, placing the ring in the middle of her palm. "The jeweler helped me after that. It's not much, but—"

"I love it," she blurted. Tears glistened in the corners of her eyes as she held the ring close to her chest and made a small, choked sound. "I would have taken a tin ring from a gumball machine from you, Lyle. You didn't have to do this."

"I only wish I could give you more, Jules." Taking her hands, I slipped the ring onto her finger. Much to my relief, it fit perfectly. "I know I don't have much now, but I'll bust my behind to give you everything I can."

"What more could I possibly ask for? You've given me everything that matters."

Coming from my wily coyote, those words meant the world. Julia had given me more than a prosthetic arm. She'd given me a new lease on life and a second chance. With no words adequate to express how I felt, I pulled her into my arms and kissed her.

We were going to be a family, and there was no better Christmas gift for a hound who had finally learned a new trick.

EPILOGUE

LYLE

*J*ulia paced the living room like a caged tiger at the circus, walking an imaginary groove in the hardwood floor.

"Are you sure you don't want a hospital?" I asked for at least the third time, probably pissing her off.

"I don't need a doctor! I want my midwife!"

We'd had this discussion before a few times. Maybe I'd appreciate going to the hospital, but I was cool with deferring to her preferences because she was the one doing all the hard work of birthing our twins.

"She's on the way," I assured her. "Sasha was over at Ian's house, so she's coming over with Leigh. That's what you wanted, right?"

"Yes," she groaned, only to go motionless. She stood with her eyes closed, back stiff, and jaw thrust out.

Contraction. Less than five minutes since the last one according to the clock.

I walked with her, inside and outside the house, both of us barefoot as we made a circuit through the yard. Sometimes she wanted me to hold her hands, and at other times, I rubbed her back. Then there were times when she snarled if I so much as breathed on her.

Multiples were risky for humans, but all our shifter pals claimed it wasn't unusual or dangerous for our kind. I wouldn't know. Mama was human, and a doctor had delivered me, but I trusted Julia's judgment on the matter. After all, she'd been a twin, her and Charles both born at home on the reservation.

At the height of her misery, the secondary members of her support system arrived—Leigh and Sasha took over and gave me a break to work out my anxieties on the porch with Ian, Taylor, Jada, Dani, Russ, and the kids. Mama served us sweet tea and pie that I couldn't enjoy while fretting over Jules.

My wife had been in labor all morning and most of the previous night. She'd slept little, tossing and turning whenever the contractions sent pain rippling across her back and belly.

"Man, I'm doing awful in there," I muttered.

"Trust me, you're not," Russ said. "Dani was just as snarly, believe me, and we only had one baby each time."

Dani shot her husband a dirty look.

"Just wish I could do something for her, you know? The contractions are every minute now."

"You are," Ian said. "You're here when she needs you."

"He's right," Taylor agreed. "And in a few moments, when she's done talking to Sasha and Leigh, she's going to need you again."

"I know."

Damn, she was tough. And I admired her beyond words for putting our children before any need for pain medication. I wouldn't judge her at all if she caved in though.

Nurse midwife Lani Douglas, a sorceress experienced in human and shifter deliveries of all kinds, arrived from Houston an hour after our call. I lingered with the guys for a moment longer until Leigh appeared at the door and beckoned me inside.

Along with the rest of the additions to our home, we'd created a bigger, better living room area to also double as a playroom for our twins at the back of the house. It was there that the women had created a clean environment for the birth. I arrived to find Julia on her elbows and knees on the floor, using pillows to support her upper body while Sasha held one of her hands. She'd stripped out of all her clothes, and I couldn't help but take a moment to admire her.

I finally understood what that unconditional love stuff was about, because even sweating, miserable, and in agony, she was as beautiful as she'd been the first day I realized I needed her to be mine.

"She's ready," Lani explained as Sasha and I swapped places.

"What happens now? Uh, I mean, aside from the obvious part."

"She begins to push with the next contraction. *My* role is to facilitate a safe birth for you and the twins," Lani said in the soothing tone of a voice infused with magic. We had chosen her because she promised a tranquil, natural experience during the birthing process without drugs. "So I always ask my patients if they prefer to catch the child themselves, or if they'd like me to do it. It's whatever is comfortable for you, Julia."

"I…I think I want to."

"All right. There'll be some down time between births. I've seen twins arrive as soon as four minutes after their sibling, or as late as twenty. During that time, you can skin to skin and bond with your first little one and nurse if you choose. For the pain, I'll provide a minimal amount of magical assistance as needed if you request it."

Julia nodded but her eyes closed, and she dipped her head forward again to groan.

It was time. Sasha was in the room somewhere behind me dimming the lights, Julia's supportive friend and our medical backup if anything went wrong.

Please, God, don't let anything go wrong.

Women may have been having babies since the dawn of time, but the what-ifs scared the shit out of me. I'd read about every kind of potential complication, but Lani had assured me she was able to deliver breech babies if one of the twins changed position on us between the births.

"Time to push again," Lani coached her.

Everything I could think of to say to her sounded so trite and trivial, but then I remembered what Ian said. It wasn't. If it made Julia feel better, it was worth saying. "You can do this, Jules."

On the fourth contraction, the baby crowned.

I helped Julia sit up and smiled at her while dabbing the sweat from her brow. The strain showed on her features, in her tense jaw and flushed cheeks.

"One more push," the midwife said.

Julia tightened her left hand around mine and bore down, then reached down between her legs to catch our child with her right. I didn't care what anyone said. Childbirth may be a natural part of life, but as far as I was concerned, my wife was Wonder Woman.

"It's a boy!" Julia announced before scooping him up against her chest. He was all gray and pink with a dark mop of black hair. "Lyle, it's Elijah!"

While she cradled our firstborn, I stroked her back and leaned over for a better look at his face, resting on my knees to her right. He had her small nose. "Good job, baby. God, look at him. He's so little."

Elijah barely cried more than a few, barely audible whines before he found her nipple and quieted, satisfied with receiving his first meal. I touched the top of his silky head with my flesh and blood hand, resting the other arm around Julia's shoulders.

"You did so good, Jules. You ready to do that again?"

"I don't have much of a choice." She sniffled and looked up at me. "I love you."

"Love you, too. All three of y'all."

We had fourteen minutes with him—interrupted only by me cutting his cord—before our little girl was ready to meet us. Fourteen precious minutes for Julia to rest between the births, and then she did it again, impressing every one of us with her strength.

Leigh ran to tell the guys that the second baby was on the way, while Sasha and Lani took over Elijah's care.

At first, I held both of her hands while she alternated between squatting and rocking to deliver the second twin.

Charlotte joined us with a healthy squall, already a demanding little thing who fussed at Julia's breast until she squirmed her way up for her meal. Our little girl squeezed one tiny fist around my finger and refused to let go.

Lani and Sasha helped us adjust our positions after Charlotte's cord was cut and she was bundled up. I scooted behind Julia and drew her back against my chest, supporting her while she held both children.

I glanced up at Lani and grinned. "So now what happens?"

The midwife chuckled. "The hard part is over. Once Julia passes both placentas, I'll help her get cleaned up. Her birth plan indicated she'd like to wait a few hours before the babies have their baths. If you want me to remain for that, I will. Otherwise, I trust Sasha can help her."

"You don't have to stay for this bit," Julia murmured to me.

"Hey, my family happens to be here, so you'll have to kick me out if you want me to leave."

"But—"

"I'm cool," I assured her. "I know how to look away while you and Lani do your thing."

I'd watched enough videos to doubt it would gross me out. Besides, that entire zone down there was their space. I'd decided to remain clear of anything below her waist long before Julia's water even broke last night.

Focusing on the babies instead, I watched them both nuzzle into her bare breasts. Elijah had taken his fill already and was happy to focus on our faces.

"They're so beautiful."

"Charlotte has your hair." Julia grinned down at our little redheaded princess.

Leigh poked in for a moment. "As soon as you're all settled, you have a welcoming party waiting for these little guys. I've never seen Peggy so excited or anxious."

"They better have gifts," I said, grinning at her.

"Why don't you take them out to say hello," Julia suggested in a tired voice.

"You sure?"

"Yeah, you can skip the messy bit and show them off. I know your mama would love that."

As we began arranging pillows behind her to take

my place, Julia cried out and almost doubled over again. "Is passing a placenta supposed to hurt like this?"

"No. Definitely not," Lani said. She placed her hands over Julia's round stomach as it trembled, then her eyes widened. "There's another baby here."

"What?!" we both cried in unison.

"Her labor isn't over," Lani confirmed. "There's another little one in there."

"B-b-but it's supposed to just be twins!" Disoriented, I blinked at her and willed the world to pop back into focus. Adrenaline surged through my body, tingling to the tips of each finger on my right hand.

"Nature decided to give you a freebie," Sasha chuckled.

I relinquished my children to the lioness shifter, and then I took both of Julia's hands again and held her.

"Lyle, get behind her and help her stand," Lani directed. "Julia, honey, we're gonna have you squat for this one, okay? The baby's in a breech position, and it'll be easier for you this way."

Julia nodded. Her red face and huffed breaths made me feel useless. As excited as I was for our children to come into the world, I wished there was a way to take away my wife's pain. My gaze darted to the newborns in Sasha's arms, their little pink faces framed by warm blankets.

A third baby. We hadn't prepared at all for a third child, buying everything double and in shades of yellow, cream, and sage green. We'd need a third crib. Another car seat.

"I'm so tired." Julia's whimpers tore at my heart.

"You're almost done, sweetheart. You're so close to being done. Then we can hold our babies, and you can finally rest."

With a low, guttural groan and three contractions, the birth resumed.

"Good, good. We've got the bottom out," Lani said. "Give another strong push, Julia."

When it all began, I'd told myself I wasn't going to look, but I stole a glance over her shoulder and looked down to see a slick baby bottom on its way out.

"Breathe, Jules, breathe. One big push."

Her face flushed red from effort, and with one great push, a third newborn slid screaming into the world.

Lani caught the baby and announced,
"Another boy."

I set my chin against Julia's shoulder and squeezed her tight. "You did it."

An hour passed by the time we'd gotten Julia cleaned up and situated with the babies in bed. The guys each came by to wish her well, bringing gifts and congratulating me with big grins.

"Triplets. Holy shit, man. Jada's already on my case about when we're going to have kids, and you had to go and knock her up with a litter?" Taylor whispered to me.

"It's not like I was *trying*." I excused his comment because I was emotionally exhausted and loved him too much to fight. Besides, I'd noticed it was just how they treated each other, and even Julia participated in teasing about their animal halves.

It grew on me and made me feel like one of the gang. Ian had jokingly teased that maybe he'd call on me one day if they needed someone with my set of skills.

I hoped he would.

"Anyway, take off for as long as you want from the shop. School's out of session, so T-Bone's going to help out and cover for you."

Their July birth had made it easy for me, too, since I'd just completed my first semester of college and was enjoying the summer break before the fall. Taylor had already promised me paternity pay for up to three months if I decided to stay home to get into the groove of caring for twins. Now that they were triplets, I'd need every day of those three months.

I smiled, wondering how a guy I used to hate had become one of my closest friends.

"Thanks, TJ."

When I returned to our bedroom, Mama was in a chair beside the bed holding Charlotte. I chuckled and sat on the edge of the bed to run my fingers through Julia's hair.

"How do you feel?"

"Like I've given birth to a litter," she teased. "I heard you and Taylor."

I grinned back at her and took Charlotte before Mama excused herself to see our guests. The guys and

their wives planned to stay for dinner because my
mother had outdone herself and made this enormous
southern feast with fried shrimp, chicken, taters, cornbread, and all the fixins'. I'd fix up plates for Julia and
me to enjoy in our quiet room.

"They're so tiny," I marveled. Tiny but perfectly
formed and developed. "Jules, we need a third name
now for this guy."

"I…I don't even know."

"How about Charles?" I asked.

She blinked up at me. "You want to name him after
my brother?"

"Yeah…"

Tears welled in her eyes, and I leaned down to kiss
her nose.

"Little Charles," she whispered, cuddling our
surprise son closer.

"I'll pick up a third crib tomorrow. Taylor said he'd
help me rearrange the room."

"Mmm, that's good." She smiled up at me with a
drowsy smile.

"Get some rest," I told her, delivering another kiss
to her cheek.

Her eyes drifted shut, and within seconds, she
was out.

Watching them all snooze while I held Charlotte in
my arms, I had to marvel at the turn my life had taken.
I made sure my boys were tucked in safely against their
mother, then I slid into the rocking chair to watch
over them.

I'd screwed up my past, but Julia had given me a future. No, I'd taken my life into my own hands, but she'd given me something more—a reason to keep fighting, to improve, and always be a better man.

She'd given me a family, and I'd never love anything more.

ABOUT THE AUTHOR

Vivienne Savage is the pen name of two best friends who write everything together. One works as a nurse in a rural healthcare home in Texas and the other is a U.S. Navy veteran. Both are mothers to two darling boys and two amazing girls.

All of their work varies in steam level, so pop by the VS website for details on which series is right for you!

Don't miss the chance to join her newsletter today.

For more information

www.viviennesavage.com

vivi@viviennesavage.com